The Trouble with Heroes

and Other Stories

To my parents
Alma and Clarence Vanderhaeghe
in appreciation for their sacrifices

The Trouble with Heroes

and Other Stories

by

Guy Vanderhaeghe

Borealis Press
9 Ashburn Drive
Ottawa, Canada
1983

The Publishers gratefully acknowledge the support of the Ontario Arts Council and the Canada Council.

Canadian Cataloguing in Publication Data

Vanderhaeghe, Guy, 1951-
  The trouble with heroes

ISBN 0-88887-929-6 (bound). ISBN 0-88887-927-X (pbk.)

I. Title.

PS8593.A52T76   C813'.54   C82-090033-8
PR9199.3.V36T76

Borealis Press Limited
9 Ashburn Drive
Ottawa, Canada K2E 6N4

Printed and bound in Canada

Contents

The Trouble with Heroes

Nothing comes easily to a man of fifty-six. Life is effort; grace, facility, hair—all have fled. A satisfactory leak is a memory. Governed by a monstrous prostate, I find myself a miserable subject, a mere adjunct to the gland. That's the least of my troubles.

I cry a good deal more than any time since I was seven.

My profession demands I never abandon hope. And yet, when I'm standing in front of a class of fourteen-year-olds telling them of—say Albert Schweitzer—I am overcome with sadness. I grieve for dotty old Albert, and for me. Yes, me.

Albert, I think, why didn't you stay home and play the organ? Write a few books, speculate about dear Jesus, cover the hausfrau regularly for reasons of mental hygiene, fork a little apple strudel? Albert, I've come to suspect there was no point in it all. According to rumours you were unhappy. For a while, of course, you were thought a sterling fellow, but there was no stampede to follow your example. No, Albert, you laboured and steamed in some dank jungle, as blue-green and dangerous as verdigris, all for nothing. They discovered you, found you out. It was inevitable, Albert. Your name is shit among the people who count, those men and women who chart the graphs of consequence. You haven't a friend among contributors to *The New York Review of Books*. Even a poor schoolteacher knows now you were a paternalistic, meddling, Christ-peddling, native-ass-kicking bwana of the old imperialistic stamp. The bastards won't let me have you as a hero. Not you, nor anybody else for that matter. Albert, the sons of bitches expect me to be the measure of all things.

With that kind of standard who wouldn't despair?

And worst of all, they've made me doubt my memories. If Albert Schweitzer was not as benevolent and self-surrendering as I remember, what of anything else? Didn't that girl smell naturally of lilacs, a distillation of her essence as fragrant as the odour of sanctity reputed to be given off by the corpses of saints? Wasn't I a hero in khaki, and didn't some stranger seeing me swing by in unison with the regiment ask God's special mercy for that brave boy who looked so young?

In the Book of Samuel we are told "the wicked shall be silent in darkness." Well, I'm not and at fifty-six I'd like to be able to think I've lived as wicked a life as the next man. There's not much time now to make up lost ground. Silent in the darkness, no.

At three in the morning I've crept out of bed, leaving a sleeping wife. I pad to the living room and for a moment stand swaying in the darkness. Imagine this, a one-armed man, jay-bird-naked man sobbing uncontrollably as he stares into the night, the blue light of streetlamps splintered by tears.

Why? Because I'm sure there is no more opportunity for heroism. Our judges are too severe. Lawrence of Arabia, it is indisputably proved, was a liar. And if Mr. Lawrence could not pass scrutiny, what of me? Without a belief in the possibility of heroism and endurance, what is left? That last scrap of dignity, a good death, is beyond reach.

For a long time I let people think that Wesley Willis Harder had lost his arm in action. This approach had its advantages. Certain females whose paths I came to cross abandoned ingrained pretences of modesty and willingly aided the disabled in brassiere unhooking, garter unsnapping and girdle peeling. While such ladies were apt to grow either impatient or reticent under the fumblings of the ambidextrous, the lack of facility with which I single-handedly attacked their under-garments brought a glisten to their eyes and filled them with a sudden surge of patriotism.

Likewise, the old boys who had been over for the first one, the "Great War" (somehow "my" war failed to achieve that elusive standard of greatness in their eyes), were willing to stand a beer for a vet who had taken the best the Hun had to offer and had lived to spit in his eye and laugh in his teeth.

In March of 1943, when I was finally released from a god-awful rehab center at Kitchener and sent on my merry way, I hadn't yet learned to feel ashamed of my imposture and pitiful bravado. True, comrades-in-arms were rotting in Japanese camps, the Second Canadian Division had visited Dieppe briefly at the expense of 907 of all ranks dead, and in a few months our boys would be springing on to the beaches of Sicily. Merchant seamen were suffocating in spills of bunker oil, or flaring, brief candles on red-hot iron decks. Young airmen on night-bombing runs were dropping out of the skies over Germany trailing smoke and glory, their screams lost in the deep, unyielding darkness.

2

But what the hell did that mean to me personally? I was twenty years old and the demob suit I had been provided with gratis by the Government of Canada didn't hang right with an empty sleeve. I was none too pleased at losing my old buddy, my left arm, and being offered in return a contraption that was all leather straps and cork and which sported a hook that could have no apparent earthly use, except as a lethal weapon in a beer parlor brawl or as an implement for hoisting hay bales. A legless wonder at the rehab center warned me it was a serious menace to life and limb. As he suggested, "To scratch your ass with a piece of equipment like that in a fit of absent-mindedness could have serious consequences."

He needn't have showed any concern for my health. A week after being set footloose and fancy-free I pitched my unaesthetic prosthetic out the train window somewhere near Sioux Lookout. If the elements have done their bit, the cork and leather straps are no more; but some-day someone will stumble on to one Christly big fishhook out there in the bush.

I preferred a neatly folded and pinned sleeve to dragging that grappling iron along. Insensible thing that it was, it was prone to snag nun's habits and goose adolescent girls in the full bloom of acne and sexual hysteria. Either victim could cause you a good deal of embarrass-ment—or worse.

But utility had very little to do with it. Self-pity caused me to cast off that devilish device. If I was a one-armed man, I was going to be a *one-armed* man. No disguises, no camouflage. My truculence as an innocent victim of a global dispute which I had no hand in precipitating knew no bounds. In any crowded public place I was likely to scratch my ear with my stump. I wanted my sacrifice visible.

What gave me the greatest bitterness was the way I had lost the limb. It was not, as I sometimes hinted, shrapnel at Dieppe that had parted us. Nor was it even carelessness on a training exercise, like Willie Kirton's, which cost him an eye with a fixed bayonet. While inglorious, that was still respectable, all in the line of duty.

No, Wesley Willis Harder went under the wheels of a private vehicle on the streets of London while on leave. At the time I was pissed to the gills and my peter still warm from a knee-shaker in an alley off a street in Holborn. The blackout may have been a boon for skirts-up furtive romances like my own, but it claimed its casualties. Stepping off the curb, I remember thinking how misinformed I'd been. Englishwomen were not "so refined as to possess neither bosom nor behind." My partner's caboose had been both ample and agitated and trying to keep a firm grip on the situation had given my knuckles a good scrubbing on a rough brick alley wall. A simple prairie boy, what did I know of sophisticated love? I hadn't even sampled the horizontal variety and here I was being impetuously introduced to the vertical. However, the lady in question was no longer an ingenue, and being as wise as she was long in the tooth, she made the best of the situation. While my slam, bam, thank you ma'am technique left her wanting, she settled for five shillings cab fare.

I suppose I was strutting, having been officially and indisputably delivered from the stigma of virginity. When I saw the two tiny beams, which were all that were permitted in the blackout, I tried to scream. I felt a terrible jarring shock at the hip but no pain. I felt my teeth snap shut, my body fold, and then I was grappling with the undercarriage of the car. I could only think, "Oh God, I'm dying in a state of mortal sin."

The car must have slid twenty feet, dragging me along under it, before braking to a full stop. Like a drowning man swept along by an undertow I twisted, lunged, and butted at the terrible force that bore me along. In those few seconds, I felt muscles shred and bones splinter. Unmercifully, however, I was still conscious and screaming when they began to pry and scrape me from under the car. I remember hearing the driver explaining to the crowd in a clipped voice, "Absolutely drunk. Right off the curb. I tried to brake. The steering mechanism went awry."

If he had been a country boy he'd have known why he couldn't control his little car. As my dad once told me, hitting a cow is nothing; nine times out of ten you walk away from a confrontation with a cow. Cows are big enough to be plowed aside, and small enough to be moved. Now a pig is a different matter. They're low-slung enough to pop your wheels up. A man who hits a porker at fifty or sixty miles an hour had better pinch his asshole and offer a prayer. He may be going over on his roof or sliding off the road and into a telephone pole. The gentleman had hit his first Holborn hog.

I spent two months in a military hospital. For some reason the bones in my legs set, but the multiple fracture in my left arm gave the army doctors trouble. At first it knit badly and an army surgeon had to break the arm again. Then it refused to heal and the threat of gangrene led to amputation above the elbow. Everyone was intent on telling me how lucky I was to be alive. An old British army orderly who had been a stretcher bearer in the First War told me that trading an arm to get back home and away from the fighting was a bargain. He had seen men gassed and was sure he would again; it was his only topic of conversation, that and racing dogs. "Drowning in piss, that's what it's like to be gassed, my lad. Choking on bloody piss with a lettuce up your arse. You're best off home."

My sentiments exactly, sir. The problem was getting there.

In time, of course, all was arranged with military efficiency and promptness.

4

But first I had to be "adjusted" to my condition. The army did not intend to return to mothers, boys any less sunny and hearty of disposition than it had received them. To that end I spent a six-month stint in a clammy country house where the damp trickled down the walls and I was encouraged by English nurses to "buck up". I harboured dark suspicions that our residence was designed to make a merciful end to us. Like malformed Spartan babes we were being exposed to the elements, subjected to the ferocity of a bone-chilling English winter, the severity of which was not mitigated in the least by low-grade, sparingly rationed coal which fizzled drearily in the grates.

Eventually, however, I was placed on a rusty hulk bound for Halifax. Along with me was a collection of human wrecks that defied imagination. Bunting through the dirty gray seas, our ship might have been a dream dreamt by a medieval allegorist, the perfect illustration of the Triumph of Death perhaps. A dream as subtle as those paintings of the fourteenth century—one of which I remember particularly from a reproduction. It depicted a rather patrician (at least bourgeois) gentleman viewing a decomposing corpse with his aristocratic fingers stopping his nose against the stench. Your future, ladies and gentlemen? Maggot shit.

A passenger liner had classes, descending from first to steerage. Our humble little boat had its classes too, dependent on disfigurement. First, there were the amputees, or as we referred to ourselves with comradely candor, the gimps. We had had legs blown off in training exercises, hands shattered by defective grenades, and a real celebrity— a parachutist whose silk hadn't opened. Fortunately (or unfortunately if you listened to him) he had hit a spongy moor. Landing on his side had saved him from the instant death that would have been his lot if he had landed feet first. But his back had been broken and his spinal cord severed. We wheeled him around deck in one of those silly English wicker wheelchairs. He kept a clutch of clippings from British newspapers on his amazing exploit in his breast pocket and was constantly thumbing through and reading them. Perhaps he was verifying the fact that he was alive.

All the gimps were a little resentful of that other class—the burn victims. It was they who attracted, even monopolized, the pity of the medical staff and crew members. Little wonder. But goddamn it, we thought, don't we hurt? Doesn't my stump burn and itch and pain and twitch? Doesn't one of those orderlies, those pricks, give a shit I can't manage to ride the crapper in a heavy sea?

The burn victims had their own esprit de corps. They called themselves fries. Sweet Jesus Murphy, I'll never forget those poor bastards.

Most were fliers and very young. They had manned the buzzing specks we had watched in the soft English skies, cheering their pursuit of prey as if it were a matter no more consequential than a dart game in a local. But now we saw the consequences close up. They were like inhabitants of another world; encased in pink, shiny scales of scar tissue, their features took on a reptilian cast, rigid and menacing. Mouths were slits, eyes were set in crinkled puckers, hands were burned so badly they had been turned into claws. Their hair had been seared away in patches, leaving solitary tufts which at the very best appeared to be coiffed Brillo pads.

The fries kept strictly to themselves and we could only imagine their conversations. I never spoke to a fry, except once.

I was moving down a dark, narrow passageway that stank of vomit when I met one of them. Surprisingly he asked me if I had a match. In the dim light his face appeared no more grotesque than an impassive tribal mask, but the soft, carefully modulated tones of his voice gave me the impression I was chatting with a talking head. When I struck the match, however, I was treated to a different sight. The face was so slick with waxy scars that it irradiated the light of the match. Where his nose should have been, two dark holes trained on me like pistol barrels. Perhaps he noticed my discomfiture because he lit his cigarette leisurely, almost letting the flame burn to my fingertips.

"Watch that," he said softly, "you don't want to burn yourself."

I dropped the match gratefully on the plates.

He drew fiercely on the cigarette and his forehead and cheekbones turned to copper.

"Colder'n a witch's tit on deck," he said.

"Yeah."

"Somebody said he seen Newfoundland last night. Won't be long before Halifax."

"I guess."

"You got anybody waiting there?" he asked, and I detected an uncertain edge and urgency in his voice.

"No," I said, "I got a long way to go yet. Saskatchewan. What about you?"

"My wife," he said. He paused and then said quickly, nervously, "Hey, buddy, I got to ask you a question. I can't tell myself. You know a guy can never tell how something looks on him. My wife always made these kinds of decisions. She won't even let me buy an overcoat myself. Says I have no taste. Very particular my wife about how I look. Admires a sharp dresser." He hesitated. "The reason I got to ask you this thing," he said, "is she's meeting the boat."

"Shoot," I prompted.

"Well," he said, "they give me a rubber nose—you know to cover that." He made a quick furtive gesture toward his face. "What I got to

6

ask is . . . would you laugh if you seen a guy wearing a rubber nose?"

"Jesus," I said, "no. I wouldn't. I don't think so."

"Goddamn it," he sobbed, "you tell the truth, you son of a bitch. What the hell do I do? Wear the fucking nose or not? Is she gonna laugh if I do and puke if I don't?"

I pushed past him. "Look," I said, "I don't know, ask one of your buddies."

As I hurried down the passageway, stumbling a little in my haste to get away from him and his tortured question, I heard him yell: "Don't you understand? I *can't* ask a fry. They'd laugh. They *got* to pretend it's a joke. For my wife, you bastard. It *ain't* no joke."

On deck the sour, salt wind scoured my face and whipped some tears into my eyes. He had been right. It wasn't long before I made out Halifax riding the gray horizon. He had been right. It was no joke.

How right it was for the returning soldier to sight landfall, his home and native land, with tears in his eyes.

The King Is Dead

November always makes me uneasy. The first snow fall reminds me that winter is inescapable. November is unkind to the imprudent; I feel a fugitive's guilt remembering unbought snow tires and an uninsulated attic.

Yet my uneasiness in November owes more to the things of the past than the present. As a boy November made me think of death and loss. Was there ever a wind as raw and searching as those winds of November 11? Or a more dreary spectacle than Remembrance Day Services? As I grew older the crowd grew thinner, the white plywood cenotaph more battered, the veterans balder, the mother of the fallen soldier frailer and, on the whole, the occasion sadder. As a boy I always hated Remembrance Day Services. But I was taken to them, every one. My mother's brother died in a night bombing run over Germany.

And of course, November is the month John Kennedy was shot. Every year television notes his passing on November 22.

Someone pontificates about his presidency. Kennedy is a little out of fashion now. The Bay of Pigs, Vietnam, the Cuban Missile Crisis, his Berlin speech are mentioned. There are film clips from Dallas.

An interviewer stops people in the street and asks them what they were doing when they heard the news of Kennedy's assassination. Everyone remembers; no one has forgotten that day.

*   *   *

That noon hour Diddly and I were hiding in the lee of the old brick school sharing a cigarette, safe from the bitter wind and teachers. It was a very cold day and it had begun to snow, not soft, fluffy, Christmasy flakes, but fine-grained snow as hard as salt that, whipped by the wind, bit your face and stung your eyes. Diddly was hunkered down with his hands pressed between his thighs to keep them warm, the collar of his thin jacket turned up around his ears and his white hair occasionally fluffing up in the wind like corn silk. He was also wearing sun glasses, not because the sun was strong, but because he was an albino and sensitive about his rabbity pink eyes.

Diddly and I happened to be together because I was at the age, twelve, when boys like to make dangerous friendships of which nobody approves. Diddly not only looked exotic and sinister with his chalk white hair and his sunglasses, he also had a reputation for petty thievery and fighting that made him irresistibly glamorous. And then again, he lived in a small shack by the tracks; his parents were on welfare, and his father hated the sight of him, maintaining that he was no "natural" son of his. All this made Diddly compellingly attractive.

"Jesus, give over with that cigarette," Diddly said irritably. "You're cooking it."

I passed the cigarette back to him and cast a quick glance over my shoulder that I hoped he wouldn't notice. I was afraid of being caught smoking on the school grounds, but I didn't want Diddly to guess this. However, I needn't have worried about Diddly; his attention was completely taken up with the cigarette. His cheeks collapsed hungrily as he sucked at it, and his face took on the aspects of a wizened old man's.

"Stupid," he said looking at me accusingly. "You cooked it."

That was when Earl Spender came around the corner of the school. He was a fat boy with a greasy cow lick, who always stood first in the class and had never lived down the fact that he had continually wet his pants in the first grade.

Diddly gave him a wicked smile and affectedly flicked the ashes off the cigarette with his little finger. "Take off, Puddles," he said.

Earl, however, was excited enough to brave ignoring Diddly. He stood in front of us rapidly shifting his weight from one foot to another, his fingers frantically busy doing something in his pockets.

"Kennedy's been shot. I just heard it on the radio after lunch— just before I left for school," he blurted out. He was so filled with his own importance at being the bearer of bad tidings that he didn't realize at first we hadn't understood. "*President* Kennedy!" he shrieked. "The President of the U.S. of A!"

"Sure, Puddles," I said. I didn't believe him.

Diddly stood up and flicked away the cigarette. The wind snatched it and showered us with sparks. "Give it a rest," Diddly said pointing to Puddle's pockets. "You exercise it too much at your age, it'll be tired when you really need it."

The school bell began to ring. Puddles ran on ahead of us toward

9

a group of girls gathered on the steps of the school, calling out happily, "President Kennedy's been shot! President Kennedy's been shot!"

"Jeez, give a listen to him would you?" Diddly said disgustedly.

"What do you think, Diddly?" I asked. "Maybe he's right?"

Diddly shrugged. It was a matter of indifference to him. He hadn't the slightest interest in what our teachers liked to call current affairs. Part of our daily routine involved students taking turns giving reports on news items. This was a response to a school of thought which held that if we became habituated to reading newspapers, sometime in the future we would become model citizens of a democracy, alert and well informed. Diddly's reports were, however, gleaned from the more colourful articles published in his father's *Police Gazette*. He kept us knowledgeable about the larger world: births of two-headed babies, nine year old mothers in the Congo, the danger of cancer from aluminum sauce pans, and bigamists in Liverpool.

"Maybe Puddles is right," I said. I was beginning to feel apprehensive, frightened.

"Ah, it's a habit of his, running off at the mouth," Diddly said.

We went into the school. Little kids from the lower grades were unconcernedly pushing and shoving each other at the water fountain, or standing by themselves with happy, dreaming looks on their faces, retreating for a moment into their own quiet worlds, the way only they can in the midst of a hubbub. Older children from the upper grades were huddled together, talking in whispers with scared looks on their faces. Evelyn, the prettiest girl in our grade, for once in her life not the centre of attention, was crying unconvincingly to prove she existed.

Routine, however, has its own imperatives, and children began to disperse into their home rooms with the final bell. Diddly and I went to our desks and sat down next to each other. A week before, to mark our friendship, Diddly had forced Arnold Sveinson to trade places with him so he could sit near me. Mr. Priebe, our teacher, hadn't yet noted the change, or if he had, had chosen to ignore it.

The moment we were settled in our seats Diddly began to carve on the top of his desk with the point of a divider. He was engaged in an ambitious work in a difficult medium, intending to produce over the course of a year a naked woman, correct in every detail as far as he could ascertain them. Her privates were to be sketched in the last day of school, he had told me, so if he was caught before then the consequences wouldn't be too severe. There was a good chance he wouldn't be caught either, because the drawing had absorbed most of his time for the past week, and as long as Diddly kept his mouth shut Mr. Priebe left him alone. They had a tacit agreement.

Diddly, suddenly remembering, looked up and said to me, "After school. Don't forget."

"I don't know, Diddly," I said. "Maybe today isn't the right day. We don't know what's going on here. Maybe we should go home after school and find out what's going on. You can never tell."

"Scared?"

"No."

"After school then." With that settled, Diddly bent his old man's head down again and set to work with a look of utter concentration on his face.

Mr. Priebe came into the room and laid his books down on his desk. Leaning forward, poised on the ends of his splayed fingers, he looked out at us. He was a young teacher and still relished command. From the look on his face, from the way his eyes were screwed up, we knew he was going to say something important. His pink scalp gleamed out from under the blonde bristles of his brush cut.

Puddles called out from the front of the room, "Mr. Priebe, did you hear? President Kennedy's been shot."

A look of extreme annoyance passed over Priebe's face. Puddles had ruined the effect of the little speech he had composed in the staff room after hearing the news on the teachers' radio. A moment, his moment, ripe with history and drama was lost.

"Thank you, Earl, for taking the words right out of my mouth," he said without even so much as glancing at Puddles. His eyes appeared to be fixed on the back wall. "Yes, President Kennedy was shot today in Dallas, Texas." Here he stopped, at a loss for words; that was all he knew. There was a scraping and shuffling of feet as people stirred uneasily in their desks. A girl named Jean, who always wore a tiny gold crucifix on a chain around her neck and never spoke, asked something quietly. It was the first time she had ever asked a question in class. The other girls always defended her shyness by saying that she wanted to be a nun, reason enough in their eyes for silence.

No one heard what she said. Priebe inclined his head ever so slightly toward her and asked, "What's that, Jean?"

"Is he dead?" she asked in a dry, scratchy voice.

"We don't know yet."

She began to cry without making a sound. From where I sat I could see this, but not many others could.

Puddles said defiantly, "I bet it's the dirty Russians. I bet a Russian spy killed him." He looked around the room as if challenging the other boys to form up behind him, ready to march on a children's crusade to Moscow.

"Could be," Priebe said thoughtfully, giving the matter his full consideration.

Someone asked if there would be a war. I looked over at Diddly. He had set aside his divider at the mention of war and was listening.

This question seemed to make Priebe angry; perhaps he sensed things were getting out of hand and he might be faced with mass hysteria if we continued on in this vein.

"Not very likely," he said sternly. "Now take out your books, you people. We've got work to do."

Diddly went back to scraping on his desk. He was a patient boy. He had a whole school year ahead of him.

I don't remember very much of that part of the afternoon which I spent in school. Our teachers made no mention of Kennedy's death; perhaps on orders from the principal. But somehow I concluded, without verification, that Kennedy *was* dead. I had no standard of comparison by which to judge the magnitude of that event; I merely understood that his death was something important. I can't say that I was overly concerned or suggest I possessed a greater sensitivity than is normal for a twelve year old boy. My predominating emotion was uneasiness. I was uneasy because at that age the binoculars through which we view the world are highly personal ones, and of a powerful magnification. Kennedy's death remained impersonal and abstracted, robbed of all immediacy, like the death of a distant relative with whom you have little contact or sympathy. But I knew that the death of a President, of a powerful man, had consequences; one of which might be war if the Russians had any hand in it. I could remember the tension of the Cuban missile crisis and the dire predictions of adults. I was deeply concerned whether or not in the next twenty-four hours I might be reduced to a cinder.

I also felt a certain clinical interest in the death itself, of which I had heard no account. My experience and imagination, however, were so limited that I couldn't even manufacture the anecdotal details that give murder its horrible concreteness, that make it real. So Kennedy's death remained in the limbo of unreality, never fully realized. And yet I felt a certain vague sense of loss, as if I had been personally cheated of something familiar and necessary. It was as if a landmark of long standing had been destroyed. Seldom noticed until gone, it leaves the casual passerby disoriented when he discovers the empty lot, the stumps, or gaping pit that marks the place where something once stood he considered fixed and immutable.

Not strong emotions certainly and, in retrospect, not equal to the occasion. But still troubling ones, which I tried to push out of mind, particularly when school was let out that Friday afternoon.

As usual, Diddly was first out of school. He was standing waiting for me on the corner. It had stopped snowing but the wind was still blowing; a piece of paper hit my ankles and ran up my legs. We walked on down the street without speaking. Diddly wasn't dressed for this weather; he kept turning around to run backwards into the wind, blowing on his fingers and stamping his running shoes to warm his toes.

12

At last I broke our silence. "Do you think he felt anything, Diddly?"

"Who? Who felt what?"

"President Kennedy."

"Well I guess he felt something. Somebody shoots you for Christ's sake, you feel *something*. It hurts."

"But if he got it—bang! right in the head. I mean would he feel it? Or would it just be too quick and everything?"

Diddly smacked me on the head with his knuckles.

"Ow! What's that? Jesus, Diddly."

"Did you *feel* it? I hit you on the head. God you're stupid. Of course you'd feel it. Couldn't help but."

I lapsed into silence again.

"Jeez, it's cold," Diddly said.

I nodded.

"What's matter with you?" Diddly asked. "Don't want to do it?" He smiled his wolfish grin. It had taken him a week to goad me into this.

"I'll do it."

"Atta boy. That's my boy." He gave me a not so playful punch on the arm. "My old partner in crime." He kept on with his banter and his punches for a block or so. It seemed to keep him warm trying to provoke me.

The rink was only four or five blocks from school. It didn't take us long to reach it. The structure had been raised in the thirties; its paint had peeled and the boards had weathered to a silvery grey. The galvanized steel roof was stained with big blotches of rust. We didn't bother with the front door, but went around to a side door. It was locked. We went to the back door. It was locked too.

"Well, that's that," I said.

Diddly looked around quickly, "No," he said, "I'll just have to use my magic key." He pulled up his jacket and drew a screwdriver out of the waistband of his pants. "Be prepared is my motto," he said.

The door was locked with a padlock and Diddly fitted the blade neatly behind the rusty plate of the hasp screwed to the door frame. He began to lever it off. With a final wrench of the screwdriver he said under his breath, "Open sez me!" The rusty screws came out of the wood with a squeal. Diddly smiled at me with satisfaction. "Just like goddamn Ali Baba," he said.

Diddly swung the door open and I went in. My eyes, unaccustomed to the darkness, could see nothing. I heard sparrows in the rafters.

"I can't see nothing, Diddly," I said.

"I'll leave the door open."

We climbed over the boards and dropped on to the playing surface.

13

Since as yet there had been no consistently cold weather it had not been flooded. The packed earth was as hard as stone under our feet.

"I'd like to get Marlene Brossman in here alone in the dark with me," Diddly said behind me with a giggle. Marlene was a highly developed and sexually precocious classmate of ours. Filled with exuberance at the thought he screeched, "Whooee!" The sparrows in the rafters took flight with a busy whir of wings and startled cries.

"Shut up!" I said fiercely. "Just shut up."

We vaulted the boards at the opposite end of the rink and entered the foyer. The door to the foyer wasn't locked—but propped open. The caretakers must have been working in there sometime during that week.

Diddly stumbled over a bench and barked his shin. Cursing, he sat down to nurse it. After a bit he began to rummage around in his pockets, "How's about a smoke?" he asked.

"To hell with a smoke. Let's do it!" I was impatient to get out of there.

"Nah, I want a smoke first," he said taunting me. He could see I was frightened.

"Do it now, or do it yourself."

"Jeez, how's about I enjoy this for a minute? I feel like I own the place." He made an expansive gesture meant to take in everything in the rink.

"I'm going," I said, starting for the door.

"Okay. Okay," Diddly said getting to his feet. "Christ, I can't carry all them bloody sticks myself, can I?"

I followed him to the senior hockey team's dressing room. "Jeez," Diddly said, sadly looking at the padlock which was more securely fastened than the other, "my old man'll kill me if I bend his screwdriver." He did bend it too, taking the lock off.

Diddly struck a match and we went into the dressing room. At some time he had taken his sunglasses off because of the darkness, and his sore, weak eyes were blinking and squeezing shut with anticipation. There wasn't much to see: a clutter of broken hockey sticks in one corner, a ratty old hockey sock by the coal stove. The stick rack was empty.

"Goddamn it," Diddly said and kicked the sock into a corner. The match went out in his hand and he had to light another. "Where are them bloody sticks?"

"Hey, let's get out of here," I said.

"There should have been a couple dozen Northlands here. I could've sold them for fifty cents a piece," he said almost crying. "Shit!"

"Come on!"

Diddly walked over to the corner and picked up the handle of a broken stick. He'd thrown the match away but in the dim light I could see him heft it like a baseball bat. "Bastard!" He swung the stick with all his might and gave the stove pipes a whack that sent them tumbling down in a shower of soot. I knew then Diddly was working himself up to an uncontrollable pitch. I'd seen him like this before.

"Let's get out of here, Diddly!" I pleaded.

He started wrestling with the cast iron stove, trying to throw it over, puffing and panting like a wild man. It was too heavy though, and he had to give up, so he gave it a few ineffectual kicks, mindful of his toes in his running shoes. Then he started looking around the room for something else to smash—but old man Herzmer's dog whining at the dressing room door brought him up short.

"What's that?" Diddly said.

"I don't know."

We stood there rigidly, staring at each other. The dog started scratching at the door and gave a little yelp.

"It's a dog," I said, relieved for the moment.

"Jesus, ain't you the master mind, Mr. Sherlock Holmes," Diddly said. He went to the door, opened it several inches and looked out. The dog tried to push his muzzle through the breach.

"It's Herzmer's dog," Diddly said.

Everybody in town knew old man Herzmer's dog. He was a black and white brindled mongrel, named Henry, who must have been nearly fifteen years old. People said it was a pity Herzmer didn't have the dog put down, but the old man, nearly as decrepit as his dog, wouldn't part with him. The two of them were a familiar sight, the dog half-blind, staggering drunkenly after Herzmer as he went scavenging for soft drink and beer bottles.

"What's he doing here?"

"He must have come in the back door and went all around the walkway. Herzmer's likely looking for bottles back of the rink where Eddy and all those high school guys drink."

"Is Herzmer around?" I asked.

"I can't see him," Diddly replied. The dog launched a long-drawn-out howl.

"Let him in, Diddly," I said desperately. "He wants in and he won't shut up otherwise."

Diddly opened the door. The dog walked to the middle of the room and lay down.

Diddly, exasperated, threw himself down on a bench. "Stupid goddamn dog. What're we going to do now?" For the first time since we had broken into the rink he sounded uneasy. "Henry, you're a stupid, goddamn dog," he told the animal. Henry, hearing his name, got up, ambled over to Diddly and stuck his nose in his face. "Go on, get out of here!" Diddly yelled, pushing him back. "This dog stinks," he said indignantly.

"He's an old dog," I said. "They all stink."

"But I mean he *really* stinks! His breath's enough to make you puke!" Diddly was trying to fend him off with a stick as the dog kept persisting in his overtures. "Bugger off!" Diddly said as Henry staggered around him, pausing now and then to thump the floor with his tail.

"Look at him," Diddly said. "He's slobbering all over enough to make you sick. Go on, get out of here you stupid mutt!" and frustrated, he gave the dog a crack on the nose with his stick. I heard a yelp, a sharp click, and then a snarl that rattled in the old dog's throat.

"He snapped at me," Diddly said surprised. Then he was angry. "The son of a bitch tried to bite *me*!"

"What do you expect?" I asked. "Leave him be."

"That's a dangerous dog," Diddly said quietly and firmly. He stood up, and began to rock on the balls of his feet like a boxer, the stick handle gently swaying to and fro in his hands like a reed in a wind.

"Oh no, Diddly," I said. "For Chrissake, let him be."

"Lousy, maggoty dog," Diddly said between his teeth.

"Let's go, Diddly," I coaxed. "Herzmer will come looking for the dog."

But Diddly wasn't listening. He began to edge toward the dog. Henry dropped down on his hindquarters, hunched his head in between his shoulders, and his snarl became tenacious and persistent. I'd seen that old dog's muzzle; it was a welter of scars and his ears were chewed ragged. He'd fight.

Diddly was muttering away to himself, talking his courage up. "I'll break his neck," he said. "I'll knock the snot out of him. I'll smash his head like a pumpkin."

"You watch him," I said. "He'll chew your ass off." I couldn't stop Diddly now; he'd made up his mind. I could only warn him. I climbed up on a bench to get out of the way. "He'll take a chunk out of you, Diddly. You think you're so smart, we'll see."

"I'll smash his head like a pumpkin," Diddly repeated.

Innumerable dog fights must have taught Henry the maxim that the best defence is a good offense, for the next thing I heard was the scrabbling of his nails on the floorboards and Diddly's stick going thwack! thwack! as the old dog lunged. Diddly must have laid a good blow along his ribs because the dog twisted abruptly, rolled, and presented Diddly with his hindquarters, his head snaking along his side to bite and hold hard. I had seen dogs do this in a dog fight, hoping to draw the other dog in and then catch him by the throat. But Diddly was no dog. He gave Henry a vicious cut across the back legs that dropped him in a bundle.

"You watch him, Diddly!" I shouted, dancing excitedly on the bench. My blood was up. "He gets a hold of you, he won't let go."

16

The old dog, however, was finished. Diddly had proved himself the boss. Henry got to his feet and favouring one of his back legs limped to the door. He had resigned; he wanted out.

Diddly was having none of this. "I'll get good lumber on the bastard this time," he said. "Just see if I don't."

"Halloaa dawg!" It was Herzmer calling in his frail old man's voice. He paused, and then again, "Halloaa dawg!"

"Christ!" Diddly said, "Herzmer!" He tossed the stick in the corner as if it had suddenly grown hot.

The dog pricked up his ears and began to cry in a desperate whine.

"Halloaa dawg!" Herzmer shouted. "Come, Henry! Henry! Henry!"

Henry gave a sharp, tentative bark. He was still hurt and confused but any moment he would set up a racket that was bound to bring Herzmer down on us.

"Jeez!" Diddly said, "Jeez oh jeez, shut up."

That's when I jumped off the bench. I acted without taking thought. In a single motion I gathered up the stick, made several long, gliding strides, lifted the stick high above my head and brought it down. I felt a jarring tug in my shoulder, and a sharp numbing sting in my palms. The stick glanced off his skull, flew out of my hands, and skittered into a corner. The dog's legs shot out from under him and he dropped on the spot. His legs kept running and his jaws snapping for some time. I didn't know how I managed to hit him so hard and cleanly.

"Halloaa, dawg!" Herzmer called.

"Oh God," Diddly said. "You've done it now. Let's get out of here."

"No," I said, "stay put. There's no way out. Herzmer's half-deaf, he couldn't have heard anything." I thought I might be going to vomit, but aside from that I was calm and thinking clearly. I was resolved not to be caught.

"Henry! Henry! Henry!"

"Why don't he shut his mouth," Diddly said. "It gets on my nerves. Sounds like he's calling a pig."

I had to roll the dog over with my toe to open the door. I slipped across the foyer and lifted my head just above the window sill. Through the glass and wire mesh I could see old man Herzmer standing in the back doorway, silhouetted against the fading light. His shoulders were slouched and his head was straining forward to see, swivelling slowly from side to side.

"He'll go away soon," I said to Diddly when I came back.

"Jesus, you did that dog good," Diddly said. "Take a look at him."

"Shut up," I said. I was furious with him. It was all his fault.

Diddly didn't bother to answer me. Perhaps he was scared of me now. We sat in the dark and listened to Herzmer call his dog for what seemed hours. He wouldn't give up. Oddly enough he didn't enter the rink to look for the dog. Probably he was afraid of slipping in the dark and breaking a leg. Old people are always terrified at the thought of falling. He just kept calling. I tried to think of something else to stop myself from hearing him, but nothing worked, not even concentrating on Kennedy's death, and wondering what might be going on.

At last Herzmer gave up and went away. Diddly and I left the dog lie. We knew we should try and hide the body but neither one of us would touch it. When we crept out it was dark and past our supper time. We ran together in the dark and cold, wanting nothing more than to get home. Diddly left me on my doorstep. I called out to his retreating back, "You were right, Diddly. He was a dangerous dog. He might've bit a little kid, and then what? When they get old they get cranky. He was dangerous."

Diddly didn't answer. He just waved goodbye.

That nonchalant wave implied no judgment of me; perhaps it was even a commendation. I knew I had risen in Diddly's estimation. But I also knew that Diddly had lost the power he had once held over me, and consequently could give no absolution.

I ate my supper in front of the television that night. Image after succeeding image pressed home the truth I hadn't been able to realize earlier. Kennedy was dead. I saw it happen. There were the details I needed to make it real, supplied by a flickering screen.

No Man Could Bind Him

And always, night and day, he was in the mountains, and in the tombs, crying, and cutting himself with stones. But when he saw Jesus afar off, he ran and worshipped him, and cried with a loud voice, and said, What have I to do with thee, Jesus, thou Son of the most high God? I adjure thee by God, that thou torment me not."

Mark 5. 5-7

At first the going was pleasant enough. The surly Galilean with the nasty nest of boils on his neck ran his little sail up smartly and caught a bit of breeze coming off the land. He ran us out briskly under a full-bellied sheet, our keel carving the bright waters and a flurry of seabirds revolving high above us, marking our progress.

I put my hot and noisome journey out of mind. Closing my eyes against the glare of the enamelled waters I indulged in a little poetic fancy, murmuring old Homer's flowing hexameters to myself. This was no stinking little fishing boat outfitted with greasy tackle (so I imagined) but the blue-prowed, taut-sailed vessel which had borne Odysseus to the dread regions of the dead. (The analogy is, of course, inexact. For Odysseus carried food for the troughs of the dead—barley and blood to nourish those faint spirits. I was a freighter of the dead: food for faint worms.)

But still . . . poetic delicacies, however underdone, were a distraction from the memory of fatiguing arguments with stupid litter bearers who twice downed the body, loudly complaining of the stench and refusing to take up their burden again without a bonus. Yet somehow our loathsome caravan had made its way to the shores of Galilee and now my brother, bound in his gravecloths, was stowed safely downwind in the Galilean's boat.

And I was as comfortable as it is possible for a two hundred and seventy pound man to be under such barbarous circumstances and under such a cruel, unrelenting sun. Above all, I was thankful for a little judicious application of scent to the sleeve of my coat, prophylactic enough against assaults to the nostrils. And a philosophic cast of mind made me realize my ordeal was almost over. I could declare with satisfaction the words of Epicurus, "The limit of quantity in pleasures is the removal of all that is painful." An honourable man, I was near to fulfilling my pledge. I was bringing my brother to the tombs of his first madness; the executor of a whim of his second and perhaps greater madness.

But in this country a Greek's luck never holds. No sooner had I begun to anticipate a change in fortune then fortune fled. The wind dropped suddenly, the sail flapped feebly several times and then dolefully wound itself about the mast. That was a signal for the Galilean. He spat over the gunwales and signed that before he took up the oar he wanted more passage money. He did this by scratching his palm and holding up three fingers cracked with labour and eaten by salt.

There is no arguing with Galileans. They are a dangerous lot, the most troublesome, violent and fanatic of Jews; the most contemptuous of Gentiles and great haters of Greeks in particular, associating us with the old King Herod whom they considered a renegade and apostate. I knew that somewhere on that smelly toad was hidden the Galilean long knife which he would not scruple to employ on a flushed, sweaty porker of a Greek like me.

With as much dignity as I could muster I attempted a nonchalant wave meant to signify assent and a patrician's disregard for bargaining. It did not have the hoped for effect. The Jew smiled knowingly and insolently, displaying a fine set of strong white teeth that appeared capable of cracking a nut; or, as was more likely in his case, of severing a knuckle joint in some Passover brawl in Jerusalem. He scrambled over me unceremoniously, took his place in the stern where he fitted the one long broad-bladed oar into the oarlock and with long, vigorous sweeps began to propel us across the lake.

In the still heavy air the sun beat down on us fiercely, so fiercely that I could imagine that the boat under this inescapable pressure rode lower in the water, and that the bleak headlands which were our goal receded into impossibility. I dipped a napkin in the lake, removed my insufferably hot wig and plastered the sopping wet linen to my bald crown.

Behind me the Jew sniggered. It is all very well for him to be amused; he knows nothing of the fickleness of the boys of Scythopolis.

I settled back to make the best of a bad bargain. It was with a touch of irony that I thought of Epicurus's admonition to Pythocles,

20

"Blest youth, set sail in your bark and flee from every form of culture." Not only was it applicable to my present state—it was also the story of my brother's short, unhappy life.

*   *   *

Let me make it plain that in referring to my brother I am not implying any blood relationship between us. It is merely a way of speaking, since he was never even formally adopted. Nor was he my father's natural son, of that I am certain. I know that when my father brought Stephen home there were rumours circulating in certain circles that he had sired him on some Jewish woman, a prostitute or market slut. This I categorically deny. My father was a man of taste and distinction, and he was not given to seeking his pleasures in those quarters among the diseased and unaccomplished. And even if he was, why would he wait thirteen years before granting Stephen acknowledgement of a kind by bringing him home? No, my brother was a Jew through and through. There has never been a moment's doubt in my mind on that score.

Stephen was a market urchin, nothing more. An orphan certainly; in all probability a bastard to boot. Of course in the Decapolis one finds Jews, a good many of them. But not many of that class—outcasts, pimps, whores and petty sneak thieves, shameless eaters of pig and unclean things. Although their own people consider them dead to God and the fellowship of Israel, they remain Jews of a kind. Ignorant and superstitious as they are, they retain enough faith to blaspheme vigorously, surely a sign of some kind of rudimentary belief.

Stephen was this kind of Jew and it is to his lack of upbringing that I attribute his later unreasoning religious fanaticism. I would even argue that he was snatched up too late. He came to be neither fish nor fowl, neither Greek nor Jew. He was something in between—an unhealthy, disturbing mixture.

My father, who was a man susceptible to impulse, brought him home as a pet and playmate for me. My younger brother, the beautiful Apollonian Nicanor had died a month before and at the time I was heartsick and inconsolable at the loss of my darling brother. My father's gesture was entirely well meant but seemed to me at the time a cruel joke. In exchange for the handsome, sturdy brother I had so loved I was offered an ugly little street rat.

Stephen, as my father named him, was a loathsome creature who spoke some unintelligible argot of the market place that he imagined was Greek; a language so distorted by Aramaic syntax that it was an assault to the ear. I decided from the moment he uttered his first barbarous, uncouth sentence that I would have nothing to do with him.

21

Everything about him I found initially disagreeable. His nose, at that tender age, was mashed as flat as any boxer's. How it came to be so, he could never recall. His legs were crooked and bandy, dwarfed by an oversized upper body which already suggested the tremendous strength that was to be his only distinction in later life. His mind was as feeble as his back was strong. He could not, however, abide to be thought simple-minded. It was typical of him to tax his brain with absurd questions, doubts, and torments he was incapable of solving.

Of course, in time, his pathetic devotion to me softened my attitude towards him. When he arrived I was at the age—thirteen or thereabouts —when every young man of any distinction of mind and breeding turns his thoughts to poetry or love. I was precocious enough to be interested in both. I wrote school-boyish poems to a very military young man with whom I was infatuated. My father had provided me with a very severe and prudish pedagogos who, though stupid, was persistent enough to prove difficult to outwit. Stephen delivered my love tokens. He was cunning enough to realize that his well-being, to a great degree, was dependent on my good will. In a short time we came to realize that our mutual comfort depended on co-operation. A grudging affection arose between us which my father mistook for brotherly fidelity.

I referred to him as "Herakles", a testament to his strength. He called me "Homer", a fillip to my dreams of poetic glory. I read him Hesiod's *Theogony*. He, untouched by the poetry and solemn mysteries attending the beginning of the world, quibbled with the creation story with Jewish exactitude, claiming it to be a lie. In return for the treasures of Greek poetry he regaled me with stories of the crude debaucheries of the amharetz, the Jewish poor and outcasts, tales which I suspect he thought would excite me. In the beginning he often pressed me to visit the women of the bazaar with him. He revealed himself most markedly as a Jew in his absurd prejudice against the finer pleasures, regarding them with distaste and preferring the ugliest woman to a clean-limbed youth. The little money which a parsimonious father allowed us seemed to him abundant riches, best spent on the women of the bazaar. Despite his urging I never joined him—perhaps out of fear, perhaps because of a more delicate sensibility. However, his forays among the unwashed grew less and less frequent as the years wore on and as he appeared to become more and more Greek.

Even now I still admit that Stephen acquired some of the habits and bearing of a Greek. Although he never developed a taste for literature he seemed willingly to accept frequent bathing and the gymnasium. As I suggested before, he was no classic beauty of splendid proportions, possessed of effortless grace and feline agility; but he was a dogged, bone-cracking wrestler of awesome courage and strength.

Watching him wrestle frightened me. It was then that I realized that there was more to him than his stupid, patient face attested to.

22

Pitted against another man his face became a focus for all his terrible energy; he revealed a rage that my father had no inkling of. He threw opponents with such violence, snapped limbs and dislocated joints so frequently that eventually no one dared test himself against him.

Even as I applauded with pudgy hands and piped the cry "Herakles! Herakles! Victor!" I was dimly aware that he was a man too uncertain of his demons to be trusted. I wondered, gazing at his ugly face, whether, like some house slaves, he harboured murderous intentions he was not even aware of, and if some day he might, in a somnambulist's trance, strangle me. I was not far wrong. At the age of twenty, having been eight years with the family and after a season of hard drinking and dissipation, he raped my sister Persephone and disappeared.

*   *   *

The Galilean ran the boat up on a gently sloping beach of shingle and made it fast by dropping his anchor, a large stone trussed up in rope like a piglet bound for market. Directly before us a path crept up the arid face of the heights, winding among dusty, bitter weeds and stunted underbrush. I presumed it led to the tombs above. Searching the scarp, I blinked into the white dazzling light of midday and wondered how I would boost my bulk up that steep and narrow track.

Meanwhile, the Galilean had begun to drag my brother's body toward the bow, intent on disembarking his cargo. It was clear from his studied disregard of me that I was to make my own way. Huffing and blowing I lowered myself over the side and splashed heavily ashore, bruising my foot on a large stone in the process.

The Galilean, disgust written on his features, staggered after me, cradling the shrouded remains of my brother. These he deposited at the foot of the trail and stalked back through the surf to fetch a simple litter he had contrived out of worn sail cloth.

Imagine my horror, surprise and disgust when he made it clear by gestures that he intended me to help bear the body to the tombs above. This I flatly refused to do, violently shaking my head. At first his murderous scowls could not dissuade me. Finally he admitted to a limited, rude knowledge of Greek. In a few words he swore to leave me to fend for myself and the corpse. I pleaded and even offered more money but he would not be bribed or cajoled. The stiff-necked oaf had decided to regard the matter as touching on principle.

It was too much. My nerves were worn raw by anxiety, exhaustion and the strain of the constant haggling and threatening so necessary to keep even the smallest caravan moving. I broke down and wept. I plumped my galled, aching buttocks down amid the rocks and dug my fingers in my eyes. It mattered nothing to the Jew. In a short time I was stumbling after him, snagged by thorns, beset by flies, balancing the mortal remains of my brother in a sweaty stupor, my breath catching hot and ragged in my throat.

I would have left the body on the beach if I had not sworn—if I had not made my silent promise. Curiously enough, I felt bound by that. At the end, it was evident he regarded me as his brother. He had professed love for me. For a childless man grown ugly, old and fat, for a man living on the ghosts of past pleasures, that meant something. I am not insensitive to anyone's pain; I have felt too much of it to imagine it best dealt with stoically. No, grief's best comfort is expression.

And I had felt grief certainly at his treachery and callous, brutal use of my sister. We all suspected where Stephen had gone; he had melted back into the disease, filth and anonymity of the amharetz. No Greek could follow him there. My father hired a man, a broken-toothed Jew to find him and kill him. But he had no luck.

Oddly enough it was I who stumbled on him, years later after he had gone insane. Here, at the very spot, in Gadara. It was the most extraordinary coincidence.

All good things come to an end. I, in time, found an indulgent father grow severe. He found my poetry bad, my morals worse. He pressed me into business. It was in connection with business negotiations for supplying Roman troops that I was sent to Gadara. My dealings were with a man who had a contract to supply meat to a Roman garrison. To this end he grazed several hundred pigs on the heights above the lake, near the tombs. But his swine and swineherds were constantly menaced by a madman, a man who had once been in his employ. This lunatic lived amid the tombs, stalking naked through his kingdom of the dead, uttering blasphemies and slashing his body with flints, carving his skin into a welter of bloodily smiling cicatrices. He had been captured once and chained, but he was so immensely strong he had torn himself free. No one dared approach him or go anywhere near the tombs.

This story was naturally one that appealed to a man of my sensibilities. A man like myself, a man who lives in the light of reason, knows that sometimes sanity is a course we choose and lucidity an acquired taste that runs counter to our nature. I wanted to see this man who had surrendered to impulse.

Of course, my host and I dared not go alone to see this prodigy. We set off with a dozen of his retainers as a bodyguard, a plate of honeycakes and a skin of wine to provide refreshment. The guards tied back their wide sleeves and knotted their skirts at their loins to give their brown limbs free play in the event we were attacked. They also armed themselves with staves.

It was late in the afternoon when we set off. Our shadows were stretched long and violet in the dust as we padded along swiftly toward

24

the cluster of luminously white-washed sepulchres glittering on the hillside.

Once amid these tombs we no longer spoke. In the presence of great holiness or madness man recognizes his limitations. Such a recognition stills idle chatter. In fact, once arrived at our destination we were uncertain about this business. How does one go about summoning a madman? The men about me were uneasy, they shuffled their feet in the dust and fingered amulets, slitting their eyes warily and searching the tombs for any trace of movement that might betray our quarry.

Many of the tombs were unprepossessing affairs, little more than burrows in the sandstone sealed with whitewashed masonry. The tombs of the rich, however, were carved directly into the face of rock which rose above us obliquely and cast us into a thick, liquid shadow which no breeze seemed capable of penetrating.

At the foot of this scarp were a few scattered and fragmented bones, the litter of graverobbers. In the summer stillness the drone of fat flies lumbering in the heavy air sounded, even in the ears of a Greek, as a sacrilege.

I do not exaggerate when I say that I smelled him before I heard or saw him. As I have intimated before, my olfactory nerves are particularly delicate and sensitive. This odour, however, was as rank, hot and troubling as the catty emanations which proceed from a lion's pen, a disquieting mixture of urine, hot fur and rotten meat. The others smelled or sensed his presence at the same moment and we turned as one body to confront him.

I did not recognize at once that the madman was Stephen. He was barely recognizable as human. His chest was crusted with stripes of dried blood and the shiny pink scars of old, self-inflicted wounds gleamed palely in the failing light. His legs were spotted with sores and his jaw was so twisted, so canted to one side I was certain it was broken. He was completely naked and his body was powdered with thin yellow dust that was streaked and channelled by perspiration.

The men about me shifted from foot to foot nervously and fingered their staves, a few presented them in the direction of the madman like wavering, admonitory fingers.

The madman took a few steps forward, paused as if he had lost some important thought, and then began to tremble convulsively.

My merchant friend touched my sleeve and gave me a knowing look, intimating that I was going to be party to some entertaining sport. "Who are you?" he called to the tomb dweller. "Are you the master of these fine houses, headman of this charming village?"

"I am Legion," he replied hollowly.

"And who is Legion?"

The madman's face contorted horribly. "I know you," he said. "I know you, pig merchant. Do not tempt. Do not tempt me."

"Who is this Legion?" my host goaded. "My distinguished visitor from Scythopolis wishes to meet you and to have the honour of your justly renowned conversation."

His attention thus drawn to me, the madman searched my face intently. His contorted features relaxed momentarily and then he sniggered. "I," he exclaimed cryptically, "am Legion, brother to the Greek, or is it brother-in-law? Legion is a snuffling pig who shares the same trough with the other pigs." He made a violent, obscene gesture and cried in a high, quavering voice, "Persephone! Persephone! She loves the bristly boar!"

I realized then who he was. If I had not such good reason to fear him I might at that very moment have attacked him with the short Roman stabbing sword I had buckled on that day.

Instead I turned to my host. "Let us take him," I said quickly. "There are twelve of us. We might capture him and put an end to him and rid you of this unclean spirit that menaces your prosperity. If your men hold him," I said bravely, "I'll gut him myself." There is no use denying it; I did not fancy myself an Achilles.

"No one would advance on him," my host said matter of factly, casting an anxious eye on the men about him. "None of these men would dare take the first step. They will protect us, but don't expect them to try and take that man. He is possessed by powerful demons with which it is best not to meddle."

I then appealed directly and desperately to the men nearest me, dangling a purse of coins under their noses. "Men," I exhorted them, "sieze this demon who haunts your tombs and defiles the bones of your dead. Put an end to this man's abominations." Rotund oratory to inflame the breasts of the simple husbandmen.

"I am Legion!" Stephen bellowed, stooping to arm himself with a jagged flint.

Our guards began to edge away from us. "He attacks! He attacks!" they cried feebly to one another.

I drew my sword and brandished it in the air with martial vigour. "Now men," I cried, "sieze him!"

"Run!" someone shouted as Stephen flung the first stone into our midst. "Run!"

The contractor precipitated the panic by acting immediately on this advice. His men flew after him and I after them, grunting horribly with effort, tears of rage and humiliation coursing my cheeks and my brother's flat, brassy laughter dinning my ears.

*   *   *

What is there to add? I did not inform my father of Stephen's whereabouts. I decided that painful, troubling memories were best not resurrected. And on reflection it seemed obvious to me that Stephen's pitiable existence was a more suitable punishment than the unimaginative death my father would hurriedly decree. Deaths are easily enough bought in certain quarters of a city, but no amount of money could buy the enduring, perpetual torture of madness. That was the retributory justice of the gods and not to be dismissed.

So the years wore on. I lived my life with studious care and a just regard for sensibility. My girth increased; I wrote poems which only old friends professed to admire; there was a succession of pretty boys, each one more spoiled, spiteful and querulous than the last; I felt a certain autumnal decline in sensation. My father died and made me a man of substance.

The only new interest of my middle years was the cultivation and patronage of magicians. For the most part they were disappointingly clever frauds, but some suggested to me that they had an artful appreciation of the arcane and invisible. The sorcerers of Egypt I found the best, although numerological wizards and Pythagorean mystics continued to hold out hope of a revelation of essence, the possibility of an abstract cosmological purity and order that transcended the disorder of flesh, bone and despair.

It was in regard to this hobby that a servant told me of a disciple of an Egyptian-trained magician who was resident in Scythopolis. The problem with kitchen fools is that they make no distinction between holy men, prophets and rabble-rousers, and dispassionate inquirers into the universal mechanisms. It was so in this case. A servant was sent to fetch me the magician and returned with Stephen.

I recognized my brother at once; he still carried the air of intensity that had struck me at Gadara, although it was obvious he had no knowledge of who I was. I had not aged gracefully, ample folds of fat, a smooth, pink pate and a jealous lover's attempt to disfigure me by slitting my nose had done little to encourage recognition on his part. The recent metamorphosis of madman into mystic only sharpened the edge of my curiosity.

I must say that I no longer felt any hate for this abject figure; long ago he had passed out of the realm of my concern. But I was interested to know a little of his perplexing journey through life and half-suspected that his sudden reappearance in my life was a sign. A Syrian astrologer would have confirmed it.

I interviewed him on my patio, seated beneath a tree cumbered with waxy-white blossoms, in a fragrant shade. He seemed hesitant to approach me and I feared for a moment he recognized me. It was soon obvious he hadn't, but still he stubbornly refused to yield his place. His great flat horny feet with their cracked nails were planted on the tiles securely.

"You, I am told," I began benignly, "are the disciple of a Jewish magic-maker. I have heard that you preach his virtues at the city gates. Tell me, what powers has your master given you government over? What secrets has he revealed?"

"He has given me dominion over nothing. I know no secrets of unearthly things," he replied testily.

"What? You have dominion over nothing?"

"Nothing."

"You must put me in contact with your master then. What does he command?"

"Unclean spirits," he said abruptly. "They are subject to him. And the Dead—they do his bidding."

The last was an old story. "I am not interested in any such tales," I said dismissively. "I am tired of stories of dead bodies which are made to plow, reap and weave at a sorcerer's whim and for his profit."

"No, no," my brother said excitedly. "My teacher does not make slaves of the dead. He sets them free from death; they regain personality, activity. They have freedom—even to sin." He paused, as if he were relating gossip or rumour which needs qualification. "Or so I have heard," he said softly, as an afterthought.

"Heard?" I said. "Heard? An old woman could say as much. A disciple must be able to say much more. A disciple must say I have *seen*."

"Heard is enough," he replied serenely.

This was amusing. "Ah! you have *heard*. But you know none of the master's secrets. It is obvious you are not a trustworthy disciple. He is afraid you will grow rich with his magic. You are not to be trusted," I teased.

The stupid oaf stared at me with his great cow-eyes.

"Answer me!" I said warmly. His stupid intractability was annoying. He didn't even attempt to refute my implied criticism. "Have you no loyalty? Are you too stupid to know his doctrine? I am told you sermonize at the gate and hector passersby. Are you dumb here? Tell me your message."

He smiled. "As I was told by him I say it simply to you," he said in the voice a child assumes for recitation. "I was possessed of a legion of devils. I lived in the tombs at Gadara and cut my flesh at their bidding. All men were afraid of me and hid from me. By the power of God I was healed and set free of my burden. I was told to tell of this up and down the Decapolis." He shrugged. "I don't know any more than that."

I was dumbfounded. "But surely this man has a doctrine," I said agitatedly. "The stupidest country sheep-chaser who sets himself up as a prophet in this God-forsaken place has a doctrine. There is some snippet of scripture he fastens on to and which his jaws need breaking before he'll loosen his grip on."

My brother studied me shrewdly for a moment.

"Very well," he said tiredly as if he had resigned himself to my disbelief, "my master is a teacher from Nazareth who is filled with God's gifts. There are rumours that he is the Messiah."

This was at last getting interesting. "And you? Who do you think he is?"

He smiled slowly, considering my question. "You do not care for an ignorant man's opinion."

"Ah," I said with a trace of asperity, "but you are not an ignorant man. We are speaking Greek, man. Tell me who you think he is."

"Moses," said my brother, "was troubled that the people would not believe he was chosen by God to lead them. He asked the Lord to give him His name so that the people would believe. The Lord knew that no name would content the people. It would be merely a thing to mumble, a charm. So God told Moses, 'You must tell them: The one who is called I AM has sent me to you.' That was a mystery which even the simpleton could consider. So an ignorant man says to you, it does not matter if I tell you the name of my teacher, or if I tell you he has performed miracles. A miracle was necessary for me. A madman denies all laws and so it was necessary. But to you I say this, He is Who He is—and that should stop your mouth. The people at the gates ask if he does what is necessary for them—if he straightens limbs, casts out devils, opens blind eyes. Ask me no questions except those necessary for you. You are a Greek and you rule—the Decapolis is yours. You need no Messiah to drive out the oppressor. It is for a Jew to yearn for the Messiah and question me if my master is the Messiah. Ask for what you need and it may be found in the God who is I AM, but do not be frivolous."

This stupid rebuke from the pious hypocrite made me heave myself out of my chair in anger.

"Men like you," I said, "find that their tongues earn them beatings. You are not speaking to your camel-dung spattered illiterates now. Use an ignorant tongue with the ignorant. Keep peace with me—my servants know how to wield a stick."

For a moment I saw the old quick anger in his eyes. "I keep no peace with Greeks," he said bitterly. "Greeks put too many things in books and then consider matters settled by arranging the alphabet."

"What do you know of Greeks to judge them?" I inquired.

"I know this much," he said. "The Greeks never keep silent—and in their noise they breed devils like manure sprouts toadstools. They wake up one morning and find out a demon has crept into their belly.

29

I know this because I lived as a Greek for a long time—a whole horde of demons crept into my belly."

I was a little surprised at the passion and conviction with which he said this. "So you attribute the growth of demons to the written word and intelligent discourse?"

"I am a Jew," he said sternly. "The Greek is taught to doubt; the Jew to believe. As a boy I grew up in the market. I earned my bread by leading the men of the caravans to the prostitutes outside the gates. I filched from baggage trains, I passed bad money, I stole. But I knew this much: without the government of God the stars would fall down. I knew I was a bad Jew because I did not keep the Law. But I knew there was Law."

"What are you saying?"

"And then a Greek collected me in the market one day," he said, apparently ignoring me. "I thought he was going to make a boy prostitute of me. But he didn't. He took me home to amuse his son." He shook his head. "That boy offered sacrifices to the gods and imagined it nothing more than poetry. Everything in life for him was something else. He lived as if nothing was punished or rewarded by God. If it were, he said, there would be no freedom. Everything was to be done for itself. This made every act pure and perfect as it related to intention. I did not understand any of this Greek business.

"In the gymnasium everyone trained very hard to make their bodies beautiful. No one ever questioned what the use of this was. The youths wrestled—not so much to win, but to provide an opportunity to display their oiled muscles. They were all afraid of my ugly, ill-proportioned body because I had understood that a man learns to wrestle to do the thing itself. I broke a lot of bones."

"And that pleased you," I said sarcastically, "to break a lot of bones?"

"Nothing pleased me then. You are a Greek and so do not understand. Do you think I cared to wrestle? It was the demon already inside me that made me break bones. I looked at those smooth faces and those heads of curls and I thought: You imagine that life is light and health and reason? No, my friend, it is also broken bones and broken teeth and tears. My lesson to these Greeks was a cracked rib or a snapped finger bone. These things are best learned young, but being Greeks they only learned to keep clear of me."

"And what other lessons did you endeavour to teach the Greeks," I said, thinking of my sister, and speculating on this madman's preposterous reasoning.

"I did not try to teach anyone anything else," he said simply. "Greeks are too cunning for me. I only tried to remember that God had made man in his image and how foolish He would be if He looked like a Greek."

"I imagine," I said dryly, "that this happy thought sustained your faith."

"No," he said innocently, "I sinned greatly—the demons ruled my penis. I sinned with Samaritan women in the bazaar. I was very frightened by the boy who I was made to call my brother. I did not understand him. I wanted him to come with me to the bazaar so he would be tempted to sleep with a woman. I felt that if we sinned together he would lose his power over me."

"And what power did this boy have?" I inquired with interest.

"He had the power to make me doubt," said Stephen. "I will never forget what he taught me to say when I was boy." He clenched his eyes shut momentarily, remembering, and then said, "The gods can either take away evil from the world and will not, or, being willing to do so cannot; or they neither can nor will, or lastly, they are both able and willing. If they have the will to remove evil and cannot, then they are not omnipotent. If they can, but will not, then they are not benevolent. If they are neither able nor willing, then they are neither omnipotent nor benevolent. Lastly, if they are both able and willing to annihilate evil, how does it exist?" His sing-song recitation ended, he regarded me soberly. "This," he said in an aggrieved tone, "was the work of a mere child. It is not natural."

"That," I said, "was the work of Epicurus, an eminently sane and reasonable man."

He shrugged. "That a child should even consider such a thing, or teach another, is unnatural. Children abide with God."

"What was that boy to do? I am certain he meant only to give you cause for thought. Perhaps he intended to strengthen your faith by challenging it." We never cease to excuse ourselves.

"That boy should not have meddled with me. I loved him too dearly. My love for him almost led me to forget God."

I was stunned by this. The words had the effect of an ear-ringing, face-stinging slap. To cover my confusion I stroked my freshly-shaved cheeks negligently and asked, "So you cared something for this Greek, then?" It was something I had never imagined, that I might engender love.

"Of course," he said sharply, "I lived as his brother. I loved him. I found him persuasive because I loved him. He made me forget the bazaar. There I had seen life that he could never know. Greeks, of course, know sorrow; I do not deny it. But when a Greek dies of a cancer he lies in a clean bed, perhaps a little incense burns on a brazier, someone holds his hand firmly. It is painful no doubt; his tears come freely and genuinely. But he has a great advantage. He can choose to die with dignity. A Greek can turn his face to the wall and die silently and heroically because his little world has gathered at the bedside to witness his departure. An old woman in the bazaar gives up the

31

ghost shrieking because she knows to die silently would be to die unnoticed. Would anyone allow that? To die unnoticed? Better to split your neighbour's ear drums—you may be lucky enough to have him kick you.

"No, you see I was happy at times to masquerade as a Greek. When my brother read me Homer I imagined that life was courage, grace and effort, death the occasion for a song to keep your memory bright. But there are no songs for the amharetz; they die unnoticed except by God. It is the poor who make God necessary and God necessary for the poor. Otherwise the Greeks would be right and the whole argument settled. Isn't that so?"

How does one answer that sort of thing? I smiled in a way which was not meant to encourage him.

"I went back to the bazaar," he continued. "Unlike my brother I knew the smell of suppurating sores and vice. I was frightened because I was ignoring God. I was beginning to doubt. My brother was as insinuating as a snake. I had to cut myself off from all that. But I knew, too, the attractions of security and a full belly. I could not run away. I decided to many times. But I was afraid and got drunk and broke more bones instead. I was weak. My flesh had known too much comfort." He pressed his lips together tightly and then he began to talk very quickly. "So I decided on a very great sin, a sin that would cut me off from all Greeks. The demons were gaining control of me. Like a Roman general I wished to burn all bridges behind me so that I might never return to this Greek world where everything was *reasonable*. I wanted also to teach those Greeks a lesson and show them that the Decapolis was not just classic pillars and plinths but also maggots and rats. I committed a very great sin. I raped the daughter of the house. I said to myself, 'This will set me free to live as a Jew and to follow the Law. There will be no choice after this but to live as a Jew. I will be a fugitive from the Greeks.' "

My heart was slowly strangling in my chest; I leaned forward in my chair, my mouth working like a fish after bait. "And did you?" I asked. "Did you live as a Jew?"

"No," he said sadly. "The amharetz cannot keep the Law. It is too difficult for the poor to keep and so they never trouble to learn it. I could not forget the sin I imagined would liberate me. In fact, once I was again cold and hungry I regretted it. 'Why,' I asked myself, 'couldn't I have chosen to keep the Law in comfort? The Greeks are a remarkably tolerant people as long as a man remains civilized about the whole matter.' But there was no turning back. Regret is a terrible thing. It makes a man bitter. I found I could not live as a Jew; it was beyond my capacity. But I had a Jew's sense of sin. A regretful man degrades himself—I took work that not even the poorest Jew would accept. I became a swineherd. I smelled pigshit until I tasted it. Do you know anything of pigs?"

"I confess a lamentable ignorance of the subject," I replied.

"Pigs," he said disgustedly. "A sow will loll on its litter, squeezing the life out of its own squealing brood. A boar will hunt and devour its own offspring. They eat anything, lizards even. Most are riddled with worms. They were disgusting—but only a little more so than the men who were their keepers, a band of outcasts and blasphemers.

"We grazed a herd of several thousand on the heights above the Sea of Galilee and I tried to keep peace with my demons. I did not still them but I kept them at bay. That is until one day.

"I was searching for a strayed boar when I came across a horrible sight. A fat, flabby sow had wandered into the tombs and rooted its way into one of the tombs of the poor where it was feeding on the corpse. From that moment the demons took possession of me. I came to believe God had ordained me as protector of the dead; I was a man left to guard the last dignity granted man, the place where I had hoped he was safe from defilement, the grave. All the demons which haunt the waste places entered into me, I had no dreams but waking dreams, I heard the dead turn restlessly in their graves, I slashed my body with stones, I chanted prayers and spied from the rocks." He paused, his lips trembling. "I knew no peace," he said softly. "I longed for the old days in my brother's house when he made me believe that pain could be borne as a crest of pride rather than a sordid humiliation. I loved my brother; he was the only person I had been granted the grace to love and now he was beyond my reach. So great was my yearning that I imagined once he came to the tombs."

"I do not understand this story," I said uneasily. "How did you come to be a follower of the magician?"

"The rabbi, Jesus of Nazareth, passed by the tombs. Whenever a stranger appeared I came out of the tombs to menace them and cause them to flee. I wanted the dead to know the peace denied me. I would not have them disturbed.

"But this rabbi did not hike his skirts and run. Instead, he questioned me, and although *I* understood the questions, the demons answered. He learned their names, since with the knowledge of names comes power over the things themselves. The demons told him they were named Legion and they begged pity that the teacher should not leave them homeless. I was afraid also because I understood the demons were part of me, and although I wanted peace I realized that the demons would leave a great empty space inside me.

"But the rabbi commanded these devils to come out of me. I felt as if I were being rent apart, separated and torn when the devils fled out of me. The master Jesus had ordered them to enter the pigs grazing some way apart and when the devils came into them, the pigs were crazed with fear. Thousands of pigs stampeded to the cliffs and toppled over, falling, falling in a snuffling, snorting, kicking, squealing cataract of flesh that plummeted into the sea and drowned, making an end of devils and grave defilers."

"And you were free?"

"Yes," he said gratefully. "I begged the teacher to be made a bondslave, a disciple of his. But he ordered me to tell of what had come to pass to me throughout the Decapolis. I pleaded for instruction but he told me only to comfort the poor with my story and to bless them with hope."

"Hope? What hope?"

"The hope of the miracle of mercy, the promise that we are relieved of despair through the agency of God."

"Nothing more?"

"One more secret," he said serenely. "This Jesus will not die. It is rumoured that already he raises his faithful followers from the dead and gives them life."

"This magician told you he will not die?"

"I told him I was afraid the demons would return, and Jesus of Nazareth promised that they would not, and that I would be with him until the world passes away."

"And so," I asked. "You have your peace?"

"There is one thing that troubles me," said Stephen. "If I die— where will Jesus find me to raise me from the dead? How will he know where to look? It is the one thing that I wonder about. Jesus will look for me at the tombs, but who will bear my body there so that he may find me?" There was such a look of agony on his face that I was forced to avert my gaze.

"That," I said, "has nothing to do with me. That would be the duty of your family."

"I have no family," he said. "As I came into the world so I will depart."

"No family?" I asked cynically. "But your dear brother whom you so loved. Isn't it his fraternal duty to see to your interment?" And I suppose regretting what I said, it was then that I promised.

*   *   *

The climb left me with nettle-stung calves, a wig askew, a sweat-sodden loin cloth. The Galilean and I poked around aimlessly until we found the tomb. He unceremoniously slung the body in.

I have repaid him for his love. I never revealed myself to him. He was correct; we had been forever separated. I dismissed him in ignorance that day; he retreated from my sunlit courtyard back into the narrow, clotted streets of Scythopolis. He knew then he was dying—he must have. In a month he was gone, from all accounts he died in the street, silently, with his face turned away from the crowd, pressed against the masonry of a wall. It was necessary for me to buy the body from his friends among the amharetz; they did not part with it gladly—but they were hungry. It was during the Jewish Passover that the transaction was concluded.

*   *   *

The sweat burned my eyes as I blinked at the blank blue sky. Some bird of prey spun high above me, turning lazily on rising currents of air. From where I stood I could not detect the wind's rush through his pinions, nor fathom the force that suspended him above the grip of the earth. Nevertheless the invisible bore him up. I never approved, but finally it was the invisible which allowed my brother to fling himself into freedom and cut the bonds of pain and necessity which bind most. Perhaps it is given only to madmen.

It is odd that I decided to keep my silent promise even when recent political rumours from Jerusalem led me to believe my brother did not predecease the magician, Jesus of Nazareth.

What would my brother have felt if it had been given him to know that master and disciple were destined to take their leave of the world together—at Passover?

Cafe Society

They made an odd trio, the three men seated around a zinc-topped table at a sidewalk cafe in the Avenue de Marigny. George Demanche, editor of *La Revue Française de l'Exploration*, was a spare, pale man who always wore his journalist's face with great seriousness. That afternoon he had chosen to top it off with an imposing silk hat, a magnificent, gleaming (yet sober) cylinder that his fragile neck appeared incapable of supporting.

The other two men gave off an air of greater solidity than did Demanche, though the impression of substantiality each one produced was of a different order. Robert Bataille, speaking forcefully at that moment, was red and beefy and loud, a gentleman with a stake in things, a proper bourgeois.

The other man, listening to him closely with a patient, if uncomprehending expression on his face, was of a different type. He sat with quiet dignity, thick, rough fingers curled laxly around his glass of beer. His cheap black coat hung awkwardly on his heavy shoulders and his beard was ragged and badly needed trimming. The man was dark too, so dark and so obviously foreign that in the year of the great Paris Exposition, 1889, with so many colonial peoples decorating the Esplanade des Invalides on the fair grounds, he could easily be mistaken for an arab, perhaps an Algerian.

"What you gentlemen are proposing is out of the question," said Bataille, shaking his ponderous head, "especially now with the Americans here in Paris."

"I suggested it might not be wise when he and Riboulet wrote me from Quebec," explained Demanche meekly. "He had ample warning." He turned to the dark man. "When was it . . . two years ago, Gabriel?"

"December of '87."

"These things cannot be mounted on such short notice," said Bataille complacently. He lifted his glass and drained it. He already had an impressive stack of saucers by his elbow.

"Yes," agreed Demanche, "perhaps you are right. In any case, I, myself, would prefer to be associated with something more educational and dignified than a Wild West Show. Lectures might be the thing. After all, it is the centennial of the Revolution . . . Liberty, Equality, Fraternity, etc. This man *is* a patriot *and* a revolutionist. What could be more topical, I ask you? There may be something in that side of him."

"They invited me to make a speech at Holyoake, Massachusetts, and once I spoke to 500 people at Woodcrest," volunteered the subject of their conversation. "In New York City I talked and they gave me a silver medal." He reached into his jacket pocket and displayed to the men at the table the bright disc shrunk to insignificance in his large, brown palm.

"Lectures mean renting a hall and publicity," said Bataille, ignoring the medal and directing his attention wholly to Demanche, "and *he* has no money for a hall. As you told me yourself, your friend is broke and living in that filthy Ternes district."

"But you see, Monsieur Bataille," said Demanche, "that is why we have come to you. We assumed that *you*, as a *distinguished* theatrical producer," he said ingratiatingly, "would raise the necessary capital for a share in the profits."

"*What profits?*" exclaimed Bataille contemptuously. "He doesn't even have a company."

"He can provide Indian chiefs and other supernumeraries from Canada on a moment's notice. This man has connections. He's respected among his own people."

"But even if he can deliver, it will be too late for the Exposition crowds, and by the time he gets his friends over here, everyone will have had his fill of savages. That American, Buffalo Bill Cody, is packing them in right now on the west side of the city." He paused. "But Paris tires easily," Bataille noted indifferently, "and by autumn, paint and feathers will be passé."

"This gentleman appeared with Cody," said Demanche, unwilling to give up. "He was a principal performer, a man of wide experience in ventures of this type."

"I performed with the Wild West Show in Philadelphia and on Staten Island," said the dark man. He laughed quietly to himself. "Son of a bitch, I rode around this little ring, around and around, shooting glass balls thrown in the air. A man feels like a fool." He shrugged. "But then again a man has to eat."

"Now that's not the sort of thing for Paris," commented Demanche, "shooting glass balls out of the air. What's needed is something more

37

refined, something historical and educational, even allegorical in nature. Liberty trampled by Tyranny might be a motif," he said judiciously, "something more to French taste."

"That American serves French taste well enough," commented Bataille. "He was certainly a hit with the illustrious President of the Republic himself, Monsieur Carnot. Cody's carnival of mock heroics has been a stunning success with all the fashionable crowd, and *he*," said Bataille pointing, "is not the kind of man to steal Cody's thunder. No golden locks. In any case, *that's* what Paris is really interested in this season." His finger stabbed at the Paris skyline. "That and Edison's phonographs in the Palais des Machines. Things, Demanche, not people. Bring me attractions like those and we can talk business."

Demanche blinked at the sight which Bataille had indicated, the new Eiffel Tower, completed that May for the opening of the Exposition. The gaunt iron skeleton thrust its pinnacle at the blue underbelly of the sky.

"That sort of drawing card we can't provide you with, I'm sorry to say," he said with a sigh.

Bataille wasn't listening. "From the moment it opened to the public this spring," he said admiringly, "it has been a hit. What a little money maker! They've all been riding up and down it—Edison, the Prince of Wales, the Shah of Persia, the Grand Duke Vladimir of Russia, even the midget Tom Thumb. There are crowds of people lined up every day for two hours to gain admittance. Paying money to scramble on that pile of scrap iron. Incredible!"

The arabic-looking man stared intently at the tower. It had puzzled him for some time now. Perhaps Bataille, who was so authoritative in all his judgments, would know. Most people only laughed and shook their heads uncomprehendingly when he asked them about it. "Monsieur Bataille," he inquired, "what's the tower thing for?"

"For?" said Bataille, taken aback.

"I mean, what is its purpose?" asked his questioner earnestly. "What I mean to say is, why was it built?"

Bataille studied the man closely for a moment to assure himself this character wasn't pulling his leg. Also, if the truth be known, he needed time to think. "Why my dear fellow," he said finally with a sly wink and a flash of his teeth, "it's there for young ladies of fashion to fly gas balloons from with their addresses attached—it's rumoured they've received answers from as far away as Switzerland! It's there to provide a restaurant in an amusing place, a situation where the nobs can eat soup and display their moustaches. It's also there for swarms of dirty little workers and their sluts to climb on for an afternoon so they can forget the miserable lives they live. In a word," he concluded, "it exists for the reason all things exist—to make money!"

38

His questioner considered this explanation. "Someone," he said at last, "told me it was built to look out for the Germans coming. It's not a bad idea."

Bataille threw back his head, hooted with laughter and thumped the table until the glasses jumped. "The mind of a bandit!" he shouted. "You've brought me an original, Demanche!"

Demanche squirmed in his chair. He felt compelled to correct the mercenary interpretation which had been offered for the construction of the tower.

"Really, Monsieur Dumont," he said, addressing the man across from him by his surname for the first time, "Robert is trying to be witty. The tower is not merely an *amusement*." He pronounced the word so that it lingered distastefully for a second on his lips. "But a triumph of Engineering Science, a symbol of man's ingenuity in treading the path of Progress." Demanche regarded the tower for a moment with evident satisfaction. "Three hundred metres high," he said. "Higher than the tallest structure ever erected by man! One hundred and seventy-five metres taller than Chartres Cathedral! A colossus! You see, Monsieur Gabriel Dumont," he said confidentially, "you are privileged to catch a glimpse of the future in that tower. It is, quite simply, a signpost for the generations to come. An achievement which they will be compelled, by example, to strive to excel."

"Ah, I see," said Dumont, nodding uneasily. It was plain he didn't see.

Bataille clapped him on the shoulder and shouted, "Don't let Demanche fool you with his romantic twaddle. That jumble of iron was piled up for money and nothing else! And the idiots are paying through the nose right this minute for the privilege of gawking off it!" He stopped to consider. "Still I'll wager you've never seen the like, not on your godforsaken Canadian plains at any rate." Bataille was growing drunk and a shade belligerent. "It takes a Frenchman to build something like that," he said, as if defying Dumont to contradict him.

Dumont closed his eyes momentarily against the sight of the black needle supported on four squat, crouching limbs. He didn't understand any of this talk. He gathered, however, that he was wrong in supposing it a lookout. It appeared it wasn't really *anything*.

Nothing done by these damn people, the French, made any sense either. They were as bad as the English who were always at you to stop wandering, to knock together a hut to crawl into, and to scrabble in a vegetable or barley patch. And when you obliged them, then they decided you'd settled down on the wrong piece of land. Why it was the wrong piece of land was never clear, especially since there was unoccupied dirt wherever you looked. And so the upshot of it all was they made a war, burned your barn, chased you to Montana, and the police confiscated your billiard table which had been shipped all those expensive miles from Ontario. It was crazy.

And now this bunch, building their Tower of Babel to prove they were something out of the ordinary. At least they had put their tower in the right place so that when God scotched it (as he was sure to) nothing decent would come to harm. Just this accursed city where the meat tasted of everything but meat, rum was hard to find, the river stunk, there were no fiddlers worth a damn, and nobody believed your stories.

Take his fellow lodgers in the grimy block of flats in Ternes. When he had told them (as it was only polite to do after listening to their stories about women and gambling) of the big fight with the Sioux on the Grand Coteau in '51, the fools in blue denim workmen's smocks had only snickered and winked and poked their callused thumbs in one another's ribs.

That had spoiled the story. For every man's story deserves respect if he does his best to tell it truthfully, and will die on his lips when it is mocked. And Dumont had wanted to get it right for them, every detail, so in this strange place, far away from the broken, rolling country where it had happened, they would feel how it had been on that glorious day. He had wanted them to see the two hundred metis carts drawn wheel to wheel, his friends in the shallow rifle pits loading and firing and calling to the Mother of God in their fear, their rifle barrels grown too hot to touch. He had wanted them to see Father Lafleche in his dirty, rusty black robes parading with a crucifix held boldly to the sky, thrust, so to speak, into the very face of God, demanding protection for his metis children.

The rattle of musketry; plunging, screaming horses sprouting the shafts of the arrows of Teton Sioux; a sky bleached white with heat; women crying and saying their beads; the Sioux dying in the grass and chanting their death songs; the old metis hunters who had sworn they could smell the blood rising from the earth like a rich, sweet mist.

A good fight! And there had been others. Duck Lake, Fish Creek, even ones that had been lost like Batoche.

"No," said Bataille emphatically, interrupting Dumont's thoughts, "you must understand, Demanche, that I'm not in the least interested despite your pleading the gentleman's cause. And I've said it for the last time. After all, who is he? What's he done that the public would care about him?"

"For the love of God," said Demanche, reddening with embarrassment.

"Oh, I'm sure he's a good fellow," conceded Bataille, jovially drunk. "Eh, you're a good fellow aren't you?" he asked, addressing Dumont. "But what did you ever do?" He fumbled for a memory.

"Why was it that Cody had you in his show? Tell me again."

"I fought Crozier and the police at Duck Lake," Dumont replied, staring at the back of his hands, "and the English general at. . . ."

Bataille drunkenly interrupted him. "Yes, yes," he said, "you shot some policemen. You know what that makes you, don't you? An anarchist!" He roared at his own joke. "An anarchist!"

"I don't know what that means," said Dumont gravely, "anarchist."

"It means that commercially speaking you are a nonentity. Nothing."

"Nothing?" said Dumont bewildered.

"There you have it," said Bataille getting to his feet. "I didn't mean to put it to you so strongly, but I'm an honest man." He looked to Demanche. "Are you coming, George?"

"Yes," replied Demanche, who wanted to flee the sight of the miserable figure in his ill-fitting coat, looking at him for all the world as if he, Demanche, were Judas.

"No hard feelings, eh?" said Bataille heartily. "And in any case, if things get really tough you may be able to sign on with the American as an extra. In the meantime, let me buy you a drink! A real drink, not that slop in your class." He beckoned to a waiter. "Hey! Bring this man an absinthe!" He rang some coins down on the table top in a grand, careless gesture and turned on his heel. Demanche tipped his hat to Dumont, smiled apologetically and thinly and hurried off to catch up with his companion. Dumont watched them make their way down the bustling pavements. As he watched them go he thought about the tower. He amused himself with the notion that with a thing like that at his disposal he could have enjoyed the pleasure of watching fat old Middleton, his red-coated militia men, and the straggling line of creaking freight wagons hump it all the way from Humboldt to Batoche. From such a height and equipped with a good spy glass he speculated he might have been able to pass the time counting the brass buttons on the General's coat. Maybe even the beads of sweat strung on his quivering jowls. It was, after all, a good idea to always keep the enemy in sight.

When Bataille and Demanche reached the curb at the corner they paused to let a landau pass before crossing the Avenue de Marigny. Bataille took the opportunity provided by this halt to say to Demanche, "I must implore you not to bring your strays around to see me anymore. I haven't the time."

"I tried to dissuade him when he wrote from Canada, but he came anyway. What was I to do? And the British have treated him very badly. I do have some sympathy for him."

"I save all my sympathy for primitives who wriggle," said Bataille, "like the Javanese and Tahitian dancers at the Exposition. I suggest you do the same."

Despite himself, Demanche broke into laughter. Bataille was vulgar, but there was no denying he was a real card. The two men comradely linked arms and strode across the Avenue de Marigny. When they reached the other side, Dumont saw them hesitate for a moment. They appeared undecided as to which way to go. Then they turned toward the Eiffel Tower as if it were a terrestrial lighthouse, a beacon by which they could unerringly steer their course down the boulevards.

The eyes of the hunter eventually lost sight of them, even after he had got to his feet, in an unfamiliar forest of brave silk hats and a bright cloud of fashionable parasols.

Lazarus

The villagers hear the first dim sounds of the procession, muffled by the heat, distant. Then, the piercing notes of the flutes, trembling and shrill, pricking the air: at last; the words of the song, the Song of Songs.

> What is this coming up from the desert
> like a column of smoke,
> breathing of myrrh and frankincense
> and every perfume the merchant knows?

The bridal party crests the hill that marks the boundary between the country and village. Here on the summit they pause as the bearers shift the poles of the bridal palanquin on their shoulders, making adjustments for the descent. Behind the procession, on the plain, are fields of barley; an occasional cypress scars the bright horizon with an austere, vertical line. No bird wheels in the sky, nothing distracts their eyes from the precipitous rush of sky to earth until the cypresses, like stitches, bind the blue with the dun. Before them there is only disorder, a jumble of houses, a tangle of streets. But here there is also life, and the streets are ripe with the bitter odours of domesticity.

For the watchers at the outskirts of the village this break in the procession symbolizes a bride's indecision: this or that? backward or forward? So when the litter resumes its progress, swaying forward, borne triumphantly and resolutely by a brightly coloured human surf, the villagers rush to welcome the bride and applaud her choice.

All but one man, Lazarus, who stands apart from the others, who is somehow distinctive. Like the rest, he has stood for hours intently waiting; but he is not a man given to running and shouting. Instead, he watches the people cast seeds before the litter and sing, and he searches

43

their faces. He is lean and spare, an ascetic perhaps. He stands with his head craned forward. The lower half of his face is covered by his cloak, so that his sharp eyes are dominant; he resembles a great bird poised to strike. Everything about him is bird-like: his frailty, his barely subdued eagerness, the way his body remains motionless while his head flickers and turns, watching.

The procession is at the village now, at the mouth of the narrow street where Lazarus stands. He can see the bride clearly, carried as she is high above the crowd on her litter. Her brown eyes shine behind her veil, her black hair is bound in wires of gold, it glistens with oil. The dust of the roadway, stirred by many feet, rises in a fine cloud about her. The crowd forces its way into the street and Lazarus is thrust against a wall by the rush.

> Your two breasts are two fawns,
> twins of a gazelle,
> that feed among the lilies,

they sing.

The litter is so close that if he desired he could reach out and touch it. As his hands trace the rough masonry of the wall, searching for a point to brace himself against the press of the crowd, he catches the scent of spikenard. He closes his eyes, almost reels with excitement as he breathes the rich odour. An image rises behind his closed lids. His sister, dark and serious, bends as she anoints the rabbi. The room fills with the heady aroma of spikenard, the shadows drink it in, the guests stir uneasily, feeling something has passed.

His eyes open. "Messiah!" he cries to the tumult. No one hears; his words are lost in the happy song and the dry rumble of many throats. He struggles to breach the crowd, to insinuate himself between the stubborn bodies, to find the face. But he is an old man with little strength, and he can only swirl feebly at the edges of the crowd.

And then he realizes that the spikenard comes from the perfumed bride who rides above him. The girl seems, for a moment, to turn toward him. She laughs, and her eyes, darkened with kohl, seem to take pleasure in his deception. But she is innocent of any malice; she laughs with joy and the wisdom of her choice.

They are past. The commotion winds through the streets, making for the house of the bridegroom, the noise shifting with every turning. Lazarus tightens the cloak across his face, attempting to mask the perfume that lingers in the air with dry, dusty wool. The street is empty now except for a crippled dog who trots, hindquarters askew, in search of the procession. Lazarus turns his attention back to the hill and gazes anxiously at it. He sees nothing, it bobs and shudders in the heat haze.

"Come quickly," he whispers. "I am waiting."

The hill answers back with nothing.

"Come," he pleads. His lids close against the glare. The scent of spikenard is still present. Is this a sign? Like the dog, he turns and trails the wedding party with faltering steps.

*   *   *

It is the second day of the wedding celebrations. The vows have been said beneath the *chuppah*, the canopy, and now the guests are feasting. The aroma of roast kid and dark honey is everywhere, even in the courtyard where Lazarus sits alone in the swiftly falling darkness.

In moments, the stars will swing up in the heavens.

There is a sprinkling of laughter from the house, the lamps are lit. But Lazarus is not drawn to these comforts. He is condemned to wait, a standard which never flutters in the breeze, a point of flesh that is a bearing for the Messiah. The demon told him so.

It happened like this. Eighteen years before the demon had visited him. Lazarus lived alone; his sisters were dead, Martha carried off by a fever years before, and Mary, only months in the grave, killed by a tumour that had swollen her belly to the size of a large basket. The quiet house had been broken, its peace gone; for Lazarus the only pleasure in life that remained was his studies. That night, however, he had fallen asleep over his scrolls and his head lay amid curling parchment.

Seeing him asleep and weakened, the tiny demon of Bethany had perched on his shoulder and whispered into his ear.

"Lazarus," he whispered urgently. "Poor Lazarus! Searching for answers on these dry skins.

"Lazarus the Scholar, that's what the people of Bethany have named you. I hear them call you that while I am in the streets going about my business. Mine is a small precinct so I get to know my charges intimately, all of them. I observe them closely, and I must say that I know none better than I know you, Lazarus. I've taken a special interest in you and your problems, and I know that you're puzzled, and I know why. From the very moment you stalked out of that tomb you've wanted to know why you were raised from the dead, and to what purpose. Of course, you realize you're an extraordinary man, perhaps one of the most extraordinary ever born. You were raised from the dead, you've seen both worlds. You're the great interpreter.

"But why were you given life? You've asked yourself that question many times. Because He loved you? Really, do you think your merits earned you such a love? I don't think so and neither do you. Were you raised from the dead to ease your sisters' grief, to wipe away their tears? What a macabre notion! What joy is there in seeing a dead man's bones jig, or in smelling death whenever you are within sniffing distance of

45

your brother? No, a rabbi of such great power could have taken away their grief in a way that didn't defy the laws of nature, that didn't flout the very statutes of creation. No, these aren't the answers.

"Well, why then?" asked the demon, shifting himself on his perch and puffing himself up. "I know the answer, and I'll let you in on the secret because I've grown fond of you after all these years, and because I believe you deserve to know your fate. You, Lazarus, were chosen to be the eternal man, the man who could never die. All around you men will wither, dry up, and blow away. But not you, Lazarus. Oh no, you will remain, for you see, you've escaped the bondage of death.

"Why? Because when the Messiah comes again he will need a witness. Very likely everyone who once knew him will have died. For this reason you were liberated from death, so that in the fullness of time you might identify him. And what a witness! Absolutely unimpeachable! Who could ever forget a man raised from the dead? Fathers will tell their sons, 'That is Lazarus, the man raised from the dead, the man who cannot die.' And their sons will remember and tell their sons, and their sons will remember and tell their sons, and their sons will tell their sons, and so it will go. No one will ever forget. You will be the signpost of the generations.

"So you must wait, Lazarus. But wait as a man, not as a god. And there's the crux of it. You will be immortal but your flesh will be as weak as your neighbour's. You will feel pain and misery, every accretion of sorrow will bow you closer to the earth. What a prospect! Year in and year out, waiting, never knowing when the great moment will come. And when it does come, everything will rest on your shoulders, there will be only Lazarus. Only poor Lazarus, scotched and scarred by life. Only Lazarus to point and say, 'That is He! I am His witness! I am Lazarus who cannot die! I remember the face!' "

The demon lowered his mouth a little closer to Lazarus's ear. Slyly he said: "Suffering and more suffering, that is what is in store for you. With every terrible year that passes, with every terrible injury done you, you'll naturally come to hate your jailer. And who could blame you?

"You'll want revenge, Lazarus. That desire will grow and grow, until it will be the only warmth you know—this hope for revenge. To be able to punish God! That will be in your power. Think of it! And when the time comes, when the Messiah appears, the people will turn to you, Lazarus, the eternal man, and ask, 'Is this one the Messiah?' Then what will you do, Lazarus? I think I know. I can forsee the outcome. Your lust for revenge will be so boundless you will deny him. You will point your finger at the Saviour and cry, 'Impostor!' And then the mob will turn and rend him, limb from limb, because their hopes will have been crushed again. The people will avenge their dreary history of charlatans and fakes.

46

"Can you imagine such a thing? You, virtuous Lazarus, a traitor to God, a traitor to man. Humanity doomed because of your hatred. Because, after all, how many times can God submit himself to such indignities?" The devil paused. "What more can I say? I've warned you. Do your best," he chuckled. "Husband your strength and your will. Spend it like a miser. He may come tomorrow or in an eternity."

And then the demon climbed down from Lazarus's shoulder and stole away before he could wake. He was the demon who sows despair and doubt, the liar and seducer, the familiar of Judas. No sooner was he gone than Lazarus awoke, filled with terror. At first he thought he had been dreaming but his shoulder ached where the demon had perched on it, and the demon's bestial odour pervaded the house. Lazarus lit a lamp and searched the corners of the room, even peered under his table, hoping to discover the demon and take him captive. He had questions he wanted to ask him. But his search was fruitless, the demon had disappeared. Where he had gone to Lazarus couldn't possibly know.

It was months before Lazarus could arrive at a decision. He begged the demon for another meeting, a short colloquy, during which he could probe his intentions. Demons, it went without saying, could not be trusted; they laid complicated snares to trap the foolish. But then again might the demon unwittingly have revealed the truth? A rich man, Lazarus reasoned, sometimes proffers to a beggar a coin of greater value than he intends. On the other hand, was this a trap to ensnare Lazarus in his own pride, and then, finally, cause him to despair and lose hope? Or had this little devil underestimated his victim, and in plotting his future thereby warned him and given him the strength to bear its vicissitudes?

And if the Messiah desired an ally could Lazarus allow himself to be found wanting? Or again, was he being led into an error that would undo him? Could any man believe that he was indispensable to the Messiah? The demon's words rattled in his ears. He was being forced to cast his lot, to enter a wager that he felt somehow he must inevitably lose. He could not afford to resort to chance, the stakes, as the demon had pointed out, were too high. Lazarus decided that he must wait, and in waiting rule his doubt.

The decision was reached during the winter rains. It seemed fitting to him that he should take up his post of vigilance outside the village of Bethany in a nasty squall, standing alone in bursts of wind and slashing, cold rain. The Messiah would come, even though no man, and he least of all, knew the hour of His coming. That was a matter of fact; it had been promised. So there he waited, as the seasons and years turned on the treadmill of his desire. There were always strangers whose faces had to be searched for a spark of divinity. Tanners that smelled of dung, drovers and shepherds, merchants from the East with spiked beards and rings in their ears, lepers and cripples. Every man who passed the silent figure, his body still quivering with anticipation after so much disappointment, had to be examined.

Yesterday the wedding had meant many strangers and an excess of hope. The scent of spikenard had drawn him here to this courtyard; it had seemed a sign. He had searched the faces, daring to believe, but had found nothing but masks of flesh, undifferentiated and unremarkable.

So now Lazarus sits in the dust of the courtyard and prays. Or is he merely speaking to himself? No matter—he is sure he is overhead.

"Answer me one question," he demands. "Why are You hiding Yourself? Need I remind You of a promise You made once to come again, soon? I know the anwers to that one, after all I was, once, something of a scholar. I don't need to be reminded that an eternity in Your sight is little more than the blinking of an eye. Very well, that's fair. But what about me? After all, an eternity is to me just that—an eternity. My bones are aching with waiting. I'm hungry for my reward. I need a little rest.

"You insist on staying hidden. Now a man cannot play hide and seek with God. I can't ferret You out. I've got to sit and wait. What's more, this monstrous game can only be terminated by one of the players. So hurry up!

"Well that may be as it is. As you know, I'm here in Bethany waiting. Whatever the reasons or the outcome I'm here. I hope there's some virtue in that. Do as you will, here I sit."

Lazarus is finished speaking. He shifts his weight and settles his haunches more comfortably in the dust. He thinks wryly of how thin he has grown. Perhaps his buttocks will leave an impression in the loose soil resembling the hoofprint of a cow.

At this moment, two men flushed with heat and wine step outside the house to catch the breeze. The taller and younger of the two, Stephen, is a member of the bride's party. Stephen has flirted with the schools at Sephoris in Galilee and has consorted with Greeks. He is a new man, a modern. He is shaved, and on one of his fingers he wears a ring fashioned with an image. At times, he thinks it unfortunate he was born a Jew. With him is Simeon, bearded and squat, a native of Bethany. The two men have little in common except that they have drunk together, and in the easy cordiality of a wedding have chosen to act the part of friends for the evening.

Stephen, dulled with wine and too much food, scrubs his face with his palms and flavours his beath with anise. Then looking around with a negligent air, he spies Lazarus, a shadowy figure, dark against the darkness, his body slumped forward, his head drooping over the earth.

Stephen nudges Simeon and asks: "Who is that man?"

Simeon strains his eyes at the purple, waving shadows. At last he recognizes him. "Lazarus," he answers. Simeon is not interested in so familiar a figure.

"Why is he sitting in the darkness, so still?"

Simeon smiles. "Old Lazarus is Bethany's madman. He's waiting for his dead rabbi." He pauses doubtfully. "At least that's what I've been told."

"Ah," breathes Stephen, curious now. "A holy man?"

"Hardly. As I said, he's merely mad. One of those who act strangely to give the impression they are sanctified. They despise and hate other men, thinking that their extraordinary behaviour finds favour with God."

Stephen, intrigued and eager to impress his new friend with the skills of controversy acquired at Sephoris, wishes to question this provincial holy man. He says: "An interesting type. I'd like to speak with him."

Simeon snorts derisively. "Speak with him? A man like him? He's old, worn out, mad, living in another world. What could he say? Anyway, he talks with no one. It's a wonder he hasn't taken to the desert."

"How does he live?"

"Who knows? Likely he eats with the dogs. Or feasts on air. Perhaps he is a sorcerer who conjures up his bread." This last thought makes Simeon uneasy; he fingers an amulet that wards off the evil eye.

"How was he driven mad? What provoked this?" Stephen gestures vaguely toward Lazarus slumped in the courtyard.

"Whatever it was is forgotten now—if anyone ever knew. My father once said he came back from the dead, although that is scarcely credible. I can remember when he was a scholar. It is likely that too many letters, too many words, addled his brain."

A roar of laughter, a snatch of music, is heard from the house. Stephen turns, and can see, through the open window, people dancing. He turns his attention back to Lazarus. "Better to be dead," he says, "than to sit in the dust and watch life pass you by."

"It won't be long either," Simeon replies, "before he will be dead. The man is a walking ghost. The spirit is staring from his eyes. And his end will be no better than was his life. There'll be no prayers for the dead, no mourners, no tomb ready to receive him. They'll drop him in a hole outside the village—just like that, into a pauper's grave. A bad ending." He shakes his head at the notion of such an ignominious end.

"A bad ending," Stephen repeats in a murmur. They turn back to the house, as if agreed this is no talk for a wedding. The door opens

49

and pours light over them, they are bathed in the smell of meat and wine. Music quivers in the air around them.

Lazarus sits in the dust waiting. The stars have come out at last. They are so large and so bright that their vast distances, so infinite, have shrunk and become comprehensible. They are his *chuppah*, his canopy, and their light lengthens his shadow across the courtyard. Lazarus is a point of stillness in the night; he is fixed, he is a stele of flesh.

Tonight with the sky pressing down upon him pitted with brilliant light, Lazarus feels for a moment that past and present is bound within his flesh and bone. He rules this kingdom of time as a steward rules in his master's absence. He *is* a witness.

Tomorrow of course, he will be tired, hungry, and sore. He will plead for strength to play the demon's role and doubt if he can endure.

But now in this night, he is sure it is not a bad thing to be still, to be silent, and to wait.

The Prodigal

I had no idea he was dying. My big sister, Elizabeth, wrote me a long lecture. Elizabeth lives in southern Ontario, but she makes a good stab at managing my life from that distant outpost. Once a year, generally at Christmas, I get a letter from Elizabeth written in peacock blue ink, covering several sheets of paper. It has never ceased to amaze me that after three children and a hysterectomy she has retained her girlish, vivacious ways. Rebellious at heart, her full-bellied characters slant backwards, and she refers to her husband, Harvey, as Poops.

I get the news of the Carlyle household, the season's litany of agues, grippes, and chills, and then sister gets down to brass tacks. Have I stopped drinking? I should. Any thought of marriage? It would be wise, I'm not getting any younger. Am I still painting? If so, there is a bare patch of wall over the sofa and the living-room colour scheme is blue. Since I live in B.C. a mountain scene would be nice.

But her letter which arrived in July was different. Daddy is dying of cancer, it said. For the love of God come and make peace with him before it is too late. Or you'll regret it for the rest of your life. And come sober. Remember, Daddy always meant well.

I came, and four weeks later I'm sweating in this fire trap waiting for him to die. It's the kind of hotel where you can rent a room by the hour; but they also have a discount weekly rate, very cheap. I haven't much money left. There is a big canvas waiting for me in Victoria half-covered with the best work I've done in years and I'm afraid I'll lose it. There's a woman too, a woman Elizabeth knows nothing about and wouldn't approve as a prospective sister-in-law. I'm afraid I may lose her too. There is every reason to leave and none to stay. I've paid my respects.

But I can't leave. I can't. Twice I've gone as far as the bus station, wincing under a brutal prairie sun that hammered a tender skull. I've stood in line for my freedom ticket and, at the last moment, turned away. I can't go. I think of him lying on that neurosurgery ward in the last rich heat of summer. His eyes bandaged, he lives in a blind man's world of sudden terrifying noises and utter darkness. They removed a tumour from behind his eye, "the size of a plum" the surgeon told me with wonder in his voice. But still he's dying. You can't doubt it. His face is wasted, his knuckles look as if they're on the point of erupting through the skin on the back of his hand. But he won't submit; he lingers in apprehension and I feel compelled to do the same.

Why? It has something to do with fathers and sons. What that means I'm not entirely sure. Nor is anyone else. In the last five hundred years how many forests have been felled, pulped, and pressed to paper so printing presses could jolt out somebody's thoughts on the problem? Hamlet's ghostly Dad gave him the itch to run a little cold steel through somebody. Edmund Gosse and Turgenev were sure the subject demanded a book of them. Freud, in a pre-war Vienna of high-flying gaiety and Strauss waltzes, dreamed dark dreams and decided we all wanted to murder Father and have our beastly way with Mom. Everybody tries to get a handle on it. We want to quantify the required minimum of filial piety, and chart the dim mysterious tides of blood.

Elizabeth, who had flown in two days before, met me at the bus station. There was nothing doing but we had to take a cab and go straight to the hospital. On the way, she clutched a handkerchief to her mouth and kept casting me side-long glances, trying to judge how I rated her illustration of grief. I don't mean to say that Elizabeth wasn't upset. Of course she was. It's just that on any given occasion she feels she has to express herself "correctly." I don't know how she arrived at her standards. All I can say is that they certainly are bizarre, and make a lot of people uncomfortable.

She also kept patting my hand in a big sisterly manner and repeating: "Don't worry, Tom. It'll be all right. I told him you were coming. He's tickled pink."

I hardly recognized the man I found in that hospital bed as my father. And it was more than the shield that had been taped over his eyes to restrict their movement that made him unrecognizable. I hadn't seen my father for nine years and it was hard to believe a man could change so dismally and radically. He was an old man now. The bull neck that used to pop the collar button on every one of his shirts was a scrawny stalk. He was a frame of bones, the barest foundation for a man, something sketched in by a hesitant hand. The only things that hadn't wasted and withered were his hands and head, which now appeared as monstrous, outsized appendages—a dollshop joke.

"Daddy," said Elizabeth, "I have a surprise for you."

You bitch, I thought. *So you didn't warn him.*

"What? he asked irritably. "What surprise?"

"It's Tom," said Elizabeth nudging me towards the bed.

"Hello Dad," I said.

"What the hell is he doing here?"

"Daddy!" Her voice was all girlish, affectionate reproach.

My father struggled to an upright postion in the bed, fumbling to tuck the pillows behind his back for support. Elizabeth went to help him.

"Well," my father said when he was settled, "fill me in on the last nine years. How's Michelangelo?"

The old bastard hadn't lost his sense for the jugular and he had a memory like an elephant. It was just like him never to forget that in a moment of hysterical adolescent anger, during one of those fights which were regular occurrences from my sixteenth year onward, I had declared that despite all the obstacles he could put in my way, I would someday be as "great an artist as Michelangelo." At the time I think I had just finished reading *Lust For Life*, or *The Agony and the Ecstasy*, or one of those other books of a like species that allow a Larger Public to vicariously enjoy the Torments of Genius. There's nothing like the delusions of youth. But to be reminded of them when you're paying storage on a hundred and forty-five unsold paintings and the ass is hanging out of your pants can still hurt.

"Michelangelo? As far as I know, he's still dead."

"Isn't it nice of Tom to come for a visit?" Elizabeth said brightly, trying to alter the course the conversation was taking.

"After nine years Greyhound must have fixed the bus," said my father.

I felt ashamed of my thin skin. After all, he was sick and he was tired. "Hey, Dad," I said softly, "how do you feel?"

He swung his head slowly in my direction. I saw that one side of his face and neck was puffed and swollen; when the light struck the two plastic shields over his eyes they shone with a slick and iridescent light. The eyes of a basilisk.

"Why didn't you stay away?" he asked quietly. "Is there some kind of pleasure in this for you?"

He could imagine that.

Elizabeth began to cry.

"I came to make peace," I said. "For Chrissakes let's not make t impossible."

This made him angry. "Make peace! Dance on my grave! My will is made, I don't owe you anything."

53

"Shove your precious will up your ass," I said. The long sleepless hours on the bus had caught up with me. "I got all I can expect from you. A couple of split lips when I was a kid and pitched down the basement stairs when I was eighteen."

"Yes, yes, and the money you cheated me of!" he yelled, the wattles on his neck wobbling furiously.

"Oh sure," I said bitterly, "I tricked you into paying for six months of my education. But the tap was turned off fast enough when you learned I was in art school and not the College of Commerce, wasn't it?"

"Tom, you shut up," yelled Elizabeth, "can't you see he's a sick man!"

"The big shot," muttered my father. "My big shot, alcoholic, artist son. Welfare artist is probably more like it."

"I earn my own living," I said as calmly as I could.

"Some living I bet."

"I make enough money to keep drunk," I said. "I'll say what you're thinking."

"And your hair is still half way down your back like a goddamn freak? Longer than your sister's?"

"Christ, it's down to my ass now," I said, "and to complete the picture I'm wearing a strapless, pink, organdy gown."

"Tom, leave him alone," said Liz, "so help me God he doesn't need this."

"Nobody needed this," I said. "Better things were left as they were."

"You selfish bastard," Liz said quietly. "I thought maybe if I brought you here you could see your way through to bend a little. You're still the selfish son of a bitch you always were, aren't you?"

"And you," I said, "are still the meddlesome bitch *you* always were. So the next time you get an urge to tinker in my life kindly go piss up a rope."

"That's your sister you're talking to!" my father bellowed.

And more of the same. I think I've captured the flavour. Liz may imagine herself a grande dame since she married Harvey (he owns his own business) but she's from the same stock as her dear brother, and within the family circle she reverts to type. She gave as good as she got. I was well past the point of ever expecting to be called a cocksucker by a matron invincibly encased in a foundation garment, but that's the nice thing about life—it continually surprises.

Anyway, the long and short of it was that Liz and I left the hospital in separate taxis bound for separate destinations. I booked into the cheapest hotel I could find, sought out a liquor store and hung a good one on.

That might have been that. I might have headed back to Victoria the next day towing my injured pride and asking myself, what else could I expect? But Liz is stubborn; she had no intention of having her plans for a touching reconciliation thwarted. She must have phoned every hotel in town; eventually she reached me about one o'clock in the afternoon and made it clear that she expected me down at the hospital.

"What for?" I asked. "He doesn't want to see me."

"Never mind what for. It's enough that he's going to die. The doctors expect a cerebral hemorrhage; it's only a matter of time. And if that doesn't get him, the cancer eventually will. There are mestastases in his neck and right lung. You get down here."

So I went and completed the family circle. There were no outbursts that day or on succeeding days. I suspect that Elizabeth, who was always Daddy's little snookums, read him the riot act. I for my part had no intention of stirring up any trouble. I let Liz attempt to reconcile. She did most of the talking for the next two weeks, chattering away to my father about the kids and Harvey and how they kept phoning to see how he was and to say how much they loved him. Now this wasn't true. Liz told me so. Harvey was on the phone constantly, ordering her home. It seemed he couldn't manage the kids and the business; he wanted her back in the love nest she had so precipitately flown.

"He's jealous," she said to me, crying in the hospital corridor. "Jealous of my father. Can you believe it?"

In the meantime I was managing to stay sober during the day, a minor sort of miracle for which I was almost as grateful as my sister. But during the evenings I lapsed and hit the bottle pretty hard. My nights were dreary, filled with sounds tiresome and sad. Shouts from the street when the beer parlour emptied at closing time; the regular, mechanical noise of traffic; my neighbour's dry coughing heard distinctly through the thin walls; the squeal of bedsprings and stifled cries of pleasure and desperation that pass for love in places like this. From my window I watched the street flare with neon and the beams of passing cars, my ass sticking to a vinyl-covered chair.

I drank and went over all my excuses for leaving. I wondered why I didn't, since I didn't feel what a son ought to. It's true my father's hostility had waned to civility; he even asked me if I was comfortable in my hotel. He never again said anything he should regret. Neither did I. But any damn fool knows that is not enough.

There was something else that bothered me. I had the feeling that though his eyes were masked, the picture he had formed of me was, in essentials, correct. He mightn't know I was balding on top at thirty-five, or sagging over my belt. But he must have been able to smell the stale sweat of booze and failure, and I think it satisfied him to know that he had been right all along. I was sure he could sense that the paintings

I carried in my skull never leapt to the canvas undiminished, but were built slowly with care and attention, and when all was said and done were still-born, muddled and flat. Was this why I felt so little? I didn't know.

God, how we had fought about my wanting to be a painter. He knew little enough about art; but Hollywood pictures, *The Horse's Mouth* and *Moulin Rouge*, had taught him that artists starved and suffered. My father loved the movies. He didn't love the idea of starvation and suffering. What he did love though was the idea of success. There was no heaven but success; no hell but the lack of it. My father believed in a materialized doctrine of re-incarnation; parents were reborn purged of dross in children who succeeded. It was a doctrine that each generation could confirm with better-tailored suits, finer cars, air conditioning, and underground sprinkler systems.

He was a labourer with almost no formal education. He could see no value in education as professors in the university described it: knowledge as its own end. No, an educated man was a doctor, lawyer, accountant, an engineer. A man with training, a man wise enough to barter years in an institution for higher earning power in the future. And I betrayed him by refusing to become one of these. Worse, I betrayed the family. It was as if I had spat in the face of all his effort, or as if after eons of blind evolution, a perverse reptile had climbed back into the sea determined to be a fish. And so neither understanding the other we had grown apart.

On the tenth of August Elizabeth finally returned to Harvey. He had finally broken her down. She gave me urgent, whispered instructions before departing, and then my father and I were left alone. I went to visit him every day. We never said much. Disease was wearing him down; he was usually too tired for any kind of conversation, and he often slept through my visits.

I took to carrying a sketch pad with me and drawing him while he slept. The tall, broad hospital windows admitted fine light in the afternoons. I'm a self-serving man, always have been. With some justice the woman who is waiting for me in Victoria said I could never be interested in a woman who wasn't also a good model. She said cynically that I prefer to combine business with pleasure. I can't argue with this, it's entirely probable that she is a better judge of my motives than I am myself. But I know this. As a painter I have a great many failings, but I never fail to recognize a good subject. Crudely and objectively speaking, my father was an illustration of all those Latin tags (memento mori, tempus fugit, etc.) that tersely enjoin us to keep last things in our minds and remind us of the corruption of the flesh. And I wanted to capture that.

So while my father slept I drew him, many times. I tried to reproduce the waxy, jutting nose, the two deep, harrowed lines that ran from the flanges of his nose to the tucked corners of his mouth, the two staring spheres that protected his eyes.

In a week I had a sheaf of papers in my hotel room, a series of drawings that gradually omitted detail until shading and line were enough to suggest what I wanted. His blurred outline seemed to float on the sheet. At least I flattered myself that it did.

"What are you doing?" he asked one day when he woke from one of his fitful, feverish sleeps and heard the rustling of paper and the scratch of my charcoal.

"I'm drawing you," I said.

He lay quietly for a moment and then asked, "Why?"

"Because I want to," I said.

*   *   *

A week ago I quit drinking. This was precipitated by a crisis, or rather a string of crises. My father has come to realize he is dying and has begun to unknowingly share confidences with me. This shouldn't disturb me, but it does. And being disturbed I would normally have begun to drink more, but I didn't. I'm not sure myself about my peculiar reaction to this state of affairs, but it seems I am trying to view this situation with clarity and sympathy. I read somewhere, once, that if enough holy water is sprinkled on someone they begin to believe. In my case, perhaps observing the outward forms of duty towards my father, I have begun to feel genuinely dutiful.

All his confessions to me have not really been confessions since he never intended them as such. They are all oblique, veiled. A single, casual sentence suddenly reveals him to me. Until now I had been satisfied with my judgment of him, comfortable with it. I had never believed that he could feel life as intensely as I could; in other words, I believed that he was less human than I. I would never have denied that he was human in a strictly anthropological sense, but I had been willing to assume that a simple man was incapable of sensing the horror of life. I thought that prophecy and sensibility were limited to a strict cultus, composed largely of people like myself, artists—interpreters. I drink, I told myself, because I see more clearly than most and the vision is unbearable. This was my affectation, my own personal crock of shit. I believed an affliction was required of me; my dignity demanded a severed ear or the equivalent.

"Your mother kept a nice house," he said to me one day.

"Yes," I said.

He began to cry. He felt the tragedy of starched curtains, waxed floors and freshly painted walls. He was pained by the transience of gifts of love.

57

It was then that I truly wanted to run away, to get the hell out of here.

Another day while I was sketching he asked tentatively, "Do you really make a living at this?"

"Of sorts."

"Who'd have thought somebody would buy a picture of me?" he said wonderingly.

I had wondered why he'd lain so still. He was helping me, posing. He thought I'd sell these death masks, these pictures of my father.

*   *   *

Yesterday began the last week of August and I sense that summer is almost over. Everything is on the verge of turning. Lawns and leaves are still brilliantly green but will soon wither; it is hot but the air has a clarity that owes something to autumn.

My father was momentarily better yesterday. I found him sitting up in bed, buttery sunshine spilling from the window on to his crumpled bed clothes.

He turned to me when I came into the room. "It's got to be a beautiful day," he said. "I can feel how warm the sun is." He held his hands palm upward as if he were offering me handfuls of this miraculous warmth and light.

"Yes," I said, drawing up a chair beside his bed, "it's a beautiful day. Maybe one of our last. You know what they say. Out here you have ten months of winter and two months poor skating."

"I'd like to go outside," he said. "I'd like some fresh air. This place smells too much like a hospital."

"Oh, I don't know," I said doubtfully. "I don't think they'd let you."

"Who asks permission?" He paused. "Take me," he said quickly.

I considered. "All right."

I'd been around the hospital long enough to know there was a medical equipment storeroom down the hallway. There were no drugs or medicines stored there, just a clutter of crutches, canes, and other hardware, so it wasn't locked. I pinched a wheelchair. Nobody seemed to notice I was wheeling contraband.

My father was so light, so frail that it took my breath away when I half-lifted him into the wheelchair. He clung to my neck, our first physical intimacy in twenty-five years.

I had to scout the hallways for nurses before we made our sprint to the elevators. That safely accomplished, it was no problem wheeling him past the main desk, busy with admissions and inquiries. I rattled him down the sidewalk and then veered off into the comparative solitude of the little playground provided for children on the pediatrics ward. The swings hung slack, the teeter-totters stood tipped and motionless. Only two children in a sand box sent up high cries of delight that sounded like some exotic bird's call.

I thought I heard my father laughing. "Christ," he said, "this feels good. It's the Garden of Eden."

I laughed too, with relief and pleasure. "Not quite," I said, "but there's a little grass."

"The Cisco Kid and Pancho," he said.

"What?"

"We're like the Cisco Kid and Pancho, fooling them, escaping. Remember? We used to listen to them on the radio, you and I. All the good guys had sidekicks. The Lone Ranger had Tonto, Wild Bill Hickok had Jingles."

"That was TV," I said.

"What? What was TV?"

"Wild Bill Hickok and Jingles."

"Yeah? I guess I forgot. I'm getting old. Anyway . . ." his voice trailed off.

"Anyway, what?"

"In a way, when you were small," he said, "I thought of you as my sidekick. Daddy's little man, that sort of thing. And I never stopped thinking that way. I should have. Who expects to play second fiddle forever?" He paused, this was an apology.

"Who should expect to be Michelangelo?" This too was an apology.

He laughed. "Stop this thing," he said. "I want to test my pins. I want to walk."

I helped him out of the chair. He began to wobble precariously as he scuffed off his slippers. "Barefoot," he said. "I want to walk barefoot on the grass. Where the hell's the grass?"

I held him under one arm and he wrapped the other around my waist. I led him to the tiny square of grass. We set off, feet gentle on the turf.

"You're fat," he said, squeezing my middle.

We marched up the patch of grass, swung around and marched down again. Up and down, three or four times. He stumbled once. I had forgotten he was blind. Somehow I hadn't been able to imagine that he could experience so much happiness through the soles of his feet. But he was, moving hesitantly through his own dark night.

He paused and lifted his face so the sun fell directly upon it.

"I don't want to die," he said suddenly.

"Of course not."

He stood in silence for several minutes. "Why do you hang around?" he asked at last.

"I'm not sure. I didn't always want to."

"I didn't keep up my end of the bargain," he said. "I was to kill a fatted calf, wasn't I?"

"Once more up the grass?" I asked.

"Why the hell not?"

I led him, blind man leading blind, both lost now in the strange empire of the senses. The feel of his body, that hive of stale blood and brittle bone that I supported, made me realize that once gone nothing could ever replace him. Blot a single figure in a carefully composed painting and suddenly everything is wrong, unbalanced, awry. I had blotted him out a long time ago. Had I lost some primitive balance because of that? Had he? Perhaps.

But yesterday, for once in our lives, we marched a little way together.

Parker's Dog

Four days after Parker sold the dog, Roy sobered up enough to recall that he had his few belongings at the Dream City Motel. It was there in the parking lot, on returning to collect them, that he saw the black dog again.

One glance at the animal Kliber led told roy something was very wrong. The dog was tossing its head from side to side in a blind, mechanical way, and lurching abour recklessly on its bowed, quivering legs. In the hot, vacant stillness of the empty parking lot Roy could hear the harsh, insect-like sound of its nails slithering and clicking on the asphalt.

Kliber halted the dog and forced it to its haunches. "So you're back," he said. "I had things for you to do."

Roy found that his tongue had dried up at the sight of the dog. He gazed down at the black friction tape wound round and round its muzzle, a thick nest of tape, layer upon binding the dog's jaws shut.

"What you done to Parker's dog?" he said. The words felt clumsy and heavy to him because of his tongue.

"Come now, Roy, you know he isn't Parker's dog anymore. I *bought* this fucking nazi hound. Remember? This is a two bottle dog I got here," said Kliber as he gently shook the choker chain so that it made a loose, silvery sound. "A two bottle of *whiskey* dog," he added, for the sake of precision.

"What you done to Parker's dog?"

"Roy, I've just tried to teach him his manners. That's what I've done. I've tried to teach the son of a bitch to growl at the man who gives him his meat." Kliber paused. "But he wouldn't learn, Roy, he just wouldn't learn. So Tuesday I taped his goddamn mouth shut on him. For two days now he hasn't ate or drank. Every once in a while I show him a big pile of juicy hamburg just to remind him of what he's missing, and when the miserable bastard growls at me I take it away on him."

Roy peered down at the dog, the trembling spikes of its ears, the dark, glazed eyes. "You'll kill him in the heat," he said. "He can't get his tongue out. Parker says that's how they cool themselves — with their tongue."

"Pretty soon now," said Kliber, "this fucker won't have the strength or the balls to growl at yours truly, and when he don't why I'll take that tape off him and let him have a nice, long drink of water and a whole pile of jeezly meat, raw, all he can eat. And you know what, Roy? This dumb fucking dog'll lick my hand. He'll lick my hand because that's the hand'll be giving him what he wants and needs more'n anything. He'll crawl on his belly to lick my hand. He'll be so fucking happy for the taste of meat in his mouth he'd lick my ass if *I growled at him.* What I figure, Roy, is that they're no different than humans. That's my philosophy to dog training."

"When Parker sees," cried Roy excitedly, "when Parker sees what you done to his dog —"

"Parker? broke in Kliber. "Parker's seen. Parker's a piece of shit. He'd have sold this dog for a pint of piss if it was the color of whiskey. Don't talk to me about Parker and what he's going to do. *Parker,*" he snorted contemptuously.

"Then me, then me, I'll, I'll -"

"Careful, Roy," said Kliber, lifting a skinny hand the color of oatmeal, "careful now. Don't you go saying nothing you might regret, Roy. Don't make any wild promises. That's called 'uttering a threat'. They got it one the books and it's a crime, and by Jesus if you threaten me I'll have the cops on you. I swear. Roy, I got to tell you *I* don't make any allowances for simple. So don't threaten me. If you don't like what you see here on my property, get your ass off it. You better get your junk and clear out. Understand? Just get the hell out of here, Roy."

"That dog'll die."

"Don't you worry about this dog. He's in good hands. You worry about yourself. This dog'll see the light," he said, giving a sharp tug to the leash. "Come along now, Rufus."

roy watched them move off, Kliber and the staggering, straddle-legged dog. "You call him his name!" Roy suddenly shoulted after Kliber. "Parker give him a name. His name's *Squarehead*!"

"Come along, Rufus," repeated Kliber, not troubling to look back. he opened the door to the motel office and scooted the reluctant dog in with his toe. The two disappeared from sight behind the sun glare on the plate glass window.

Roy stood for a moment, staring at the blazing window, his arms dangling slackly at his sides. Then he turned and ran heavily across the lot to number 23, the last unit in the south wing. But the room was empty, Parker was not to be discovered there. It was only much later that night when Roy returned from town with a quart of milk and a dozen eggs for the dog that he found Parker. He was sprawled on his bed, drunk. No matter how hard he tried, Roy could not rouse him to leave.

Roy's and Parker's living arrangement was arrived at for reasons of convenience. It was suggested by Parker in the Matador Room of the Dream City Motel the first night the two met. Roy, who had been laid off a CPR extra gang in B.C. in October, was kitchiking his way east, relaxing his work season drinking discipline and now endeavouring to stay drunk nearly every waking hour.

"As I understand it," said Parker. "waht you need is a warm place to shit for the winter, pardon the expression. And I got one. So why don't you put up with me?" As he made this invitation Parker split his ruined face with a smile fired by his last reserves of the old charm. "But I got to be honest with you, Roy," he continued, smiling, the very heart and soul of honesty itself. "Roy. . . that's your name, ain't it? Yeah? Well, as I was saying, Roy, you're a scholar and a gentleman, no doubt, and your conversation a pleasure. But that kind of society shit don't cut no ice with me. I'm after your pogy check."

His entire life Roy had found it a difficult thing to keep his checks out of other people's hands. He had come to expect to be cheated, had come to expect it as inevitable. But this man, it seemed, was making things plain from the beginning. He was striking a deal.

Drunk as he was, Roy attempted to give Parker's proposition the appearance of a dignified and careful consideration.

"All right by me," he declared at last.

"It's a real nice room," said Parker, "with two singles that vibrate if you put in a quarter. I don't pay no rent because I handyman for Kliber, the guy owns this place. See him?" he said, pointing to a sharp featured man with a widow's peak standing behind the bar. "The one there with a look on his face like a rat eating shit out of a shoe? That's Kliber."

On catching sight of the man Roy gave a bark of amazement. He had never in his life seen such a thing as a rat doing what Parker had described, and come to think of it, he believed Parker hadn't either. But there was no doubt in his mind that if he ever did see such a thing that rat would surely resemble the man drawing off draft behind the bar.

Roy would soon learn that his new friend Parker was never at a loss expressing himself. "Roy," he was often informed in the succeeding months, "I ought to been in the greeting card business. I got one for every occasion of the year." It was true, he had. Parker wrote them out on motel stationery as they came to him, and stashed them in an old shoe box. when he was in a good mood he would recite them at Roy's prompting, beginning, perhaps, with Christmas (Things is tight and times is hard/ So here's your fucking Xmas card!) and concluding with Easter. (Easter comes but once a year,) Jesus rse don't never fear,/ Chocolate bunnies are awful nice/ But salvation's cheap at twice their price!)

"You're a card yourself, Parker," Roy would wheeze, giggling and wiping his eyes. "Beats me how you ever think up those carzy rhymes."

"Roy," said Parker, attempting to divert his attention from Kliber by tapping the bottom of his glass sharply on the table. *"Roy!"*

"Yeah"

"You applied for the unemployment yet?"

Roy shook his head.

"Well, tomorrow we'll fix that up," said Parker. "the sooner the better, eh? Pierre'd be disappointed as hell if he knew we wasn't on his UIC drinking team, pulling our weight." He reached across the table and slapped Roy on the shoulder. *"Pull your weight, Roy, goddamn it. Do her for Team Canada!"*

"I will," said Roy, grinning and hoisting a glass.

The month before his unemployment insurance expired, Roy lived in fear that Parker would send him away. All his life he had been accustomed, one way or another, to paying for companionship, and he did not expect to be allowed to stay. When Parker told Roy he had talked Kliber into letting Roy help him with odd jobs, Roy was overjoyed.

"It's kind of like subcontracting," Parker explained. "He pays me and I pay you."

For days Roy was filled with an inchoate gratitude which he eventually tried to give expression to by clumsily making Parker's bed in the mornings. After a week of this an embarrassed Parker told him to stop.

There didn't prove, however, to be much money in subcontracting. Working for Kliber appeared to mean working for a room, food from the motel restaurant kitchen, occasional pocket money, and above all, booze. The two men might work for next to nothing, but Parker demanded security of a kind, an alcoholic's safety net. On Sundays and Mondays when the Liquor Board Store in the small town wass closed and they had nothing to drink, or if they were broke, Parker expected Kliber to supply them from his liquor stock in the Matador Room.

"You just ask? said Roy, the first time Parker demanded, and

Kliber produced, a bottle of gin.

"No worries here in Dream City," said Parker. "The well never runs dry."

Roy wondered aloud at this bounty, at Kliber's generosity.

"Don't you wonder," Parker replied. "The word charity ain't in that son of bitch's vocabulary. Kliber's so fucking mean and so fucking cheap he'd crowbar Christ off the cross to get the nails. Stop and think now, Roy. What's our room cost him? Nothing. This place is never more'n half full so he ain't losing rent, is he? No, he ain't. And he don't pay us a salary, but he's got us on twenty-four hour call. Something busts, get Parker out of bed. That's what he does.

"Don't you see, Roy? He wants to keep us around. Me especially since I can fix anything." Roy did not consider this bragging on Parker's part. You had to hand it to him, if he was half-way sober there wasn't much that could stump him. "Can you imagine the money he'd have to put out if every time something went on the fritz in this shithole he had to call a plumber, or electrician, or TV man? Plenty. He wouldn't be able to afford to buy no christly Cadillac. I know that for a fact."

The Cadillac was something that rankled with Parker. He resented Kliber owning such a car. "If he'd drive it, why that'd be different," Parker would say. "But there ought to be a law against that, like there was in the last war against profiteering." Others might find it a mystery that the car had sat in the motel parking lot under a tarpaulin for months on end, never moving, but Parker didn't. "He bought it for an investment. He won't dare drive it for fear of a scratch or scrape. When he's ready to retire he'll sell it to a collector, take his money down to Arizona and sit in the fucking sun till every bit of juice is baked out of him. Dried shit and a wallet sitting in the sun and they'll call it Kliber."

Roy did notè think Parker was right, but he never dared to oppose Parker's opinion with his own. From watching Kliber's peculiar rituals which involved the car, he did not believe that Kliber ever intended to sell it. Every Wednesday at three wekk intervals Kliber would unshroud the car, thoroughly wash it, and apply another coat of wax. Then, finished these chores, he would slide behind the whell and spend a half an hour staring steadfastly through the windshield, sitting absolutely still and absorbed. Following this strange communion Kliber always repeated to some one, anyone who would listen, and that was most often Roy, "You know, I wanted one of them as long as I can remember. I knew they built quality right into them. Take the smell. She still smells new. That's got to be some kind of record. A year old and she still smells showroom."

No, Roy knew that Kliber would never sell the car. It had taken possession of him. If Roy could have put into words what he suspected Kliber felt sitting in the car, he might have said fear. Fear of losing something long wished for, which, for a time, feels like perfection. Roy understood that desire to hang on to what had come so hard, to let nothing touch or mar it. He had learned that time brought an end to most things that were good, as Kliber knew that time evaporates the smell of newness, causes knobs to twist off in the hand, paint to flake, windows to shatter in intricate cobwebs of fracture, steel to powder into rust. Kliber, who wanted so much to *have* things, to possess them completely, was mounting guard against the first scratch that blights everything.

Roy in his slow, vague way guessed this. He understood. Roy was waiting for the first cruel word Parker really *meant*.

Because he was sitting on the walkway that ran around the second story of the Dream City Motel, enjoying the breeze, Roy could see the man and the black dog while they were still some way off, wading shakily through a slough of heat haze on crumpled, contorted legs. Glacing up a few minutes later from uncapping a beer, he recognized that it was Parker who was being dragged along by the dog bounding at the end of the short leash. On they came across the parking lot, the dog straining forward, a drunken Parker jolting along stiff-legged in an attempt to restrain it, one hand grimly holding on to the belt he had removed to make an improvised leash, the other clutching the pants he was in danger of losing.

"What you got there, Parker?" Roy hollered down to him.

"Whoa!" yelled Parker, *"whoa, you squarehead son of a bitch!"*

"There was no stopping the dog. It dragged Parker past Roy, Parker's legs flopping and his hair bouncing up and down in his eyes, and jerked him right over to Kliber's canvas-covered Cadillac. Then it lifted a hind leg and dribbled on the tarp.

"Just like a fucking German," said Parker, combing his hair out of his eyes with his fingers. "Sniff out something nice and piss on it. That's typical."

"What you got there, Parker?"

"I figure," replied Parker, "that this dog is mostly Doberman Pinscher. Maybe there's some black Lab in him too. But don't ask me for no papers. Look at him," he proudly urged Roy. "Some fucking dog, eh? All teeth and nuts."

Where'd you get him, Parker?"

"I found him in the highway ditch. Somebody must've drove off and left him at the side of the road. Let me tell you, there's some real assholes in the world." Parker reached down and began to fondle the dog's ears. It grined up at him, tongue hanging out.

"What's matter?" said Roy. "You two in love?" He laughed uncomfortably.

66

"He'll be good company for me," Parker said. "And it'd be a smart idea to have a dog around here at night, what with all the strangers a man doesn't know the least about, passing through a place like this."

Kliber did not agree it could be a good thing to have a dog around the place.

"Get rid of it." he said.

Neither Kliber nor Roy were prepared for Parker's answer. "If my dog goes, I go!" he cried passionately.

Kliber threatened to no avail, then showed signs of faltering resolve, finally gave in.

As Parker triumphantly pointed out to Roy, "All Kliber had to do is think about paying union rates for a plumber or electrician, and a look come over his face like he just passed a kidney stone."

So Squarehead, the name which the dog soon answered to, stayed. When at his drunkest, Parker used to marvel at how compatible the three of them were. As he explained to Roy, 'compatible' was his ex-wife Edna's favourite word. "You see, Roy, Edna said we wasn't. Compatible that is. So I figure as long as Squarehead or you doens't run off with some dink that wears a fur fedora and white belt and white shoes, why that means we're all compatible. Because that's what Edna done to me, and we sure as hell wasn't."

Roy was not as sure as Parker about the compatible business. He did not exactly welcome the presence of the dog. For one thing Parker fed it pickled eggs he stole from the bar. The farts were terrible. But that wasn't the worst. Somehow the dog seemed to have worked a change in Parker. Now he talked about troubling, disturbing things. *He talked about them to the dog.* Even with Roy there with him in the room Parker, sitting in his undershorts on a rumpled bed, two days of beard smeared on his jaws like ashes, a glass of rye in his hand, still chose to speak to the dog. From across the room Roy watched them closely with shallow, expressionless eyes, listened, and laughed whenever he thought it appropriate to laugh.

But he did not like it. He preferred the old Parker who told jokes and said his funny poems about Christmas and Mother's Day, and all the other holidays. He did not like the Parker who rambled on with his mouth twisted with something that was supposed to be a smile, but wasn't.

"You know, Squarehead," said Parker one night, "I finally decided what me and Roy there are. We're all day suckers." Roy laughed uncertainly. Parker did not shift his attention from the dog crouched beside his bed. "An all day sucker is the kind of drunk who sucks it back from breakfast to bedtime," he said. "He takes it regular and slow, like medicine, a little at a time all through the day. Except in the morning an all day sucker is extra sick. In the morning his hands won't do his buttons up. He needs a steadier. Isn't that so?" Parker suddenly inquired of Roy. The large, pale man with the flat, guarded eyes blinked and wound his fingers together in the face of Parker's challenge. Then he shrugged. "it's the truth, Roy," Parker said. "Parker tells the truth and Parker knows you know how sick a little soberness can make you."

Such talk frightened Roy. "Let's have a good time, Parker," he pleaded. "Let's get drunk and have a good time. Let's be happy. Don't talk like that, Parker."

"Take a little medicine," said Roy, tipping his glass against his teeth, "take a little medicine."

For Roy those rambling monologues were terrible things. He did not care to follow Parker's mind on its ironical excursions. Still, it was even worse when Parker insisted on speaking of the future. With a hopeless, desperate feeling Roy would clumsily plunge into Parker's slurred speeches in an attempt to distract him.

" 'Let's Make a Deal' is on, Parker," he called seductively. "It's your favourite. It's on."

"Yeah, let's you and me make a deal," Parker snapped. "You shut up and I'll talk."

Roy guiltily hunched his shoulders and feigned an intese interest in the figures cavorting on the slate blue screen.

"Come winter, Squarehead," Roy confided, "I'm going to start easing back. Just a bit every day, so's I don't really notice, or miss it. A man don't have to drink this much. I could get by on a little. It's whatever you're used to. You get used to a lot, you need a lot; get used to a little, you need a little. I could start eating again and put some weight back on; get my strenght up. I could be in pretty good shape by spring. Maybe I could look for a job someplace on construction, make a decent wage. In the fall I'd buy us an old car. I got a sister in Victoria we could visit, you and me, Squarehead. I got to get out of here. Another one of these christly winters'll kill me. It will. You better believe it."

Parker and his talk of the future. How Roy hated it. It seemed there was no place for him in Parker's future. He spoke only of the dog.

Somtimes, when Parker was very drunk, he neglected to feed his dog. It took to raiding the garbage cans behind the motel restaurant. Kliber warned Parker several times about the mess. Then, one day, emboldened by hunger, the dog crept into the kitchen and snatched a pork chop off the cutting board. Kliber, who did not know enough to leave a feeding dog alone, go a trouser leg shredded trying to take the meat away from Squarehead.

68

"I want that fucking nazi hound out of here!" Kliber shouted at Parker. "Today I want him out of here!"

"Look," said Parker, "he never bit you, did he? I mean even in the law every dog gets one free bite."

"There's not going to be any free bites around here! Get rid of that fucking maneater, Parker!"

"He'll cool down," Parker assured Roy when Kibler had left in a fury. "It's just that he's a little pissed off about Squarehead taking his cuff up on the one side there. But if we keep the dog locked up in the room and out of his way for a week or two, he'll come around."

They did just that for three days, keeping themselves as well as the dog out of sight. But by Sunday morning all their alcohol was gone. When shortly after nine o'clock Parker began to shake, he sent Roy to get a bottle of whiskey from Kliber.

Roy came back empty-handed. "Kliber says the room maid heard the dog barking in here last night. Kliber says we don't get nothing to drink while we still got the dog. He says get rid of the dog."

"He's fooling," said Parker, shocked. "Ain't he?"

"He means it. You know how he is when he means something."

"It's Sunday. Sunday and we're broke. Where do I get a drink on Sunday?" Parker put his head in his hands. "Jesus, I feel awful. Pretty soon I'm going to start to heave."

"I'll walk into town," said Roy. "I'll get us a bottle."

"You fucking simple shit," said Parker tiredly, without lifting his face out of his palms. *"You fucking simple shit.* Where are you going to get a bottle with no money?"

"I could borrow it?" Roy ventured.

"From who? From just anybody? Like a cup of sugar? 'Excuse me, missus, you got a spare bottle of bingo? Me and my friend are sick, see?' You're dumber'n a bag of fucking hammers, ain't you, Roy? Leave me alone, you stupid prick."

"You just hold on, Parker," said Roy. "I'll get us a bottle."

He didn't, or course. A complaint was made to the police and they picked him up knocking on doors.

"What do we do with him?" said one officer, speaking of the huddled figure in the back of the cruiser.

"No point in locking him up," his partner said. "He's harmless enough. Let's take him back to Parker. He seems to belong to him."

When Parker opened the door to Roy and the policeman, it was plain he was very drunk.

"Your friend here was bothering people," said the officer who had escorted Roy to the door. "Keep him off the streets. Okay, Parker?"

"Oh, Parker," cried Roy when he saw the dog was gone. "Oh, Parker. *What you done?"*

When Roy returned to the Dream City Motel with the eggs and milk, his only intention was to feed them to the dog, if the dog could be found. It couldn't. Kliber was keeping it in his room, continuing its instruction in manners.

Roy had given up searching for Squarehead when the dark, humped shape of the Cadillac squatting in the shadows of the motel caught his eye. He walked hesitantly over to it and slowly drew off the tarp, listening to the canvas glide with a faint whisper over the polish.

The windows, he saw, had been left down an inch or so to prevent the summer heat from blowing them out. Dangling his belt through this gap, Roy managed to hook the door button with his belt buckle and lift it up.

When he swung the door open, the heat contained in the car boiled out and struck him in the face with a gust of warmth and the mingled scents of upholstery and leather. For a moment he stood as if undecided and then he stooped and crawled into the car. First, he laced the rich nap of the floor carpet with the quart of milk. Then he stowed the eggs in various spots under the seats. One he placed in the glove compartment, two he broke and dripped into the air conditioning system. These chores finished, he softly closed the door and replaced the tarp. If he remembered correctly, the car wasn't due for another washing for two weeks.

The future, Roy was to think months later, that future which Parker had so often laid his plans for, was a funny thing. That, or something along those lines, was what ran through Roy's mind seconds before he followed the example of the man two rows down, and fumbled awkwardly to his feet to announce, to all the strange and unfamiliar faces turned expectantly toward him, "My name is Roy, and I'm an alcoholic."